TEXAS GRIT

The Adventures of
Wilder Good

#1 ***The Elk Hunt: The Adventure Begins***

"Favorites of 2013"
—Glenn Dromgoole, *Texas Reads*

"Among the best books for young boys I've seen in years. This is classic Americana, values and all." —Robert Pratt, *Pratt on Texas*

#2 ***Texas Grit***

#3 ***Wilder and Sunny*** *(coming soon)*

TM
THE
ADVENTURES
OF
WILDER
GOOD

#2

The Adventures of
Wilder Good

TEXAS GRIT

S. J. DAHLSTROM

Illustrations by Cliff Wilke

PAUL DRY BOOKS
Philadelphia 2014

First Paul Dry Books Edition, 2014

Paul Dry Books, Inc.
Philadelphia, Pennsylvania
www.pauldrybooks.com

Printed in the United States of America

Library of Congress Cataloging-in-Publication Data

Dahlstrom, S. J.
Texas grit / S. J. Dahlstrom ; Illustrations by Cliff Wilke.
pages cm. — (The adventures of Wilder Good ; #2)
Summary: Twelve-year-old Wilder Good spends a week in West Texas at his grandfather's ranch, working cattle on horseback and exploring the rough ranch country.
ISBN 978-1-58988-094-8 (paperback)
[1. Ranch life—Texas—Fiction. 2. Grandfathers—Fiction. 3. Cowboys—Fiction. 4. Christian life—Fiction. 5. Texas—Fiction.] I. Wilke, Cliff, illustrator. II. Title.
PZ7.D15172Te 2014
[Fic]—dc23

2014002976

for Livy and Annabelle—
so you may know what to look for,
and know it when you see it.

CONTENTS

Atticus said that Jem was trying hard to forget something, but what he was really doing was storing it away for a while, until enough time passed . . . When he was able to think about it, Jem would be himself again.

HARPER LEE
To Kill a Mockingbird

TEXAS GRIT

CHAPTER ONE

Momma

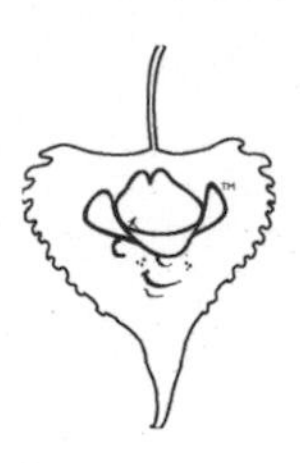

It had been a week now since the elk hunt. The cut on Wilder's leg no longer throbbed, and the stitches only felt tight. His new wound chafed against his jeans as he walked and against his sheets as he slept, and he was eager to have them out. It would make a good scar, he knew, and it was connected to a good story.

Wilder walked a little straighter, and maybe even a tiny bit slower, during school that week. He began to preface the storytelling to his friends and teachers with "You want me to tell it all . . . *again*?" unsuccessfully trying to hide his smile. By Tuesday, Sunny saw through his false modesty and rolled her eyes when he launched into the scar-showing and retelling. In some of the versions, it almost seemed that the mountain lion had actually attacked Wilder.

But his heroic week at school was over, and it was time to say goodbye to his family and go to Papa Milam's in Texas. He felt a pit in his stomach about the separation, and about his mother's pending cancer treatment in Denver. His feet dragged the floor as he got ready to leave on Saturday morning.

Livy lay lightly in the living room on the couch next to the large front window of the trailer house. The blue morning light flooded around her as Wilder walked in, and for a second he thought she was floating as all the highlights of her profile lit up with the early backlight. Anchoring her, though, he saw the chiseled creases from pain and worry in her forehead, between her eyebrows, two slight lines that never seemed to melt away, even as she rested alone. Wilder wanted to smooth them out like a piece of clay. He wanted to make them go away.

Wilder walked up to his mother and sat down with his knees against the couch and laid his head on her stomach. Her eyes never opened, but she knew he was there and she smiled and held her son as she felt the robe over her chest get hot as the boy wept.

"Why are you crying, Wilder?"

Wilder looked at his mom. She combed his hair with her fingers as he sat on the floor next to her.

"I'm just scared. I love Papa, but going down there seems so far away from you."

"Well, your grandfather is certainly rough as

a cob, I will give you that. I hate to be away from you too, son."

Livy sat up, holding Wilder's hand now.

"He is rough, but he is good. There are many things I want you to get from him."

"You want me to get some of his stuff?" Wilder dried his cheek and rubbed his eyes.

"No," Livy smiled, "I want you to learn from him. So much of life is hard, harder than you can imagine. Some of that you know already, some you don't. Your Papa knows them all, and he is still good. All men are not that way."

"Are you going to die, Momma?"

"Of course I am. You know that very well. You and I have always talked straight about everything. Let's not change that."

"When?"

"You know that answer, too. No one can know their times and days."

"Mom, why did you get cancer . . . why doesn't God fix you?" Wilder let tears roll down his cheeks again. His thin 12-year-old chest heaved.

"Wilder, you and I have been through all of that, many times. I know those questions don't go away. But those answers . . . I think you are old enough now to start wrestling with yourself. Sometimes you just have to grit your teeth and get mad and hold on. You have to hold on tight when the answers don't come easily."

Wilder stared out the window holding his mother's hands. They were so thin—that was what he always noticed now. Her skin was almost translucent, which scared Wilder. It was so different from his smooth and tanned childhood skin.

"Take your journal with you. Write about it. Write *me* a poem for once . . ." Livy smiled, "instead of all those for Sunny that nobody ever reads."

Wilder stood up in defense, yet smiled at his mom, knowing his heart held no secrets from her. He never showed her his Sunny poems, but sometimes he left them lying around, hoping she would read them.

"Poetry is dumb," he mumbled back.

"Wilder," Livy said, calmly ignoring his reply which they both knew was a lie, "I've been writing a poem in my head this morning lying here, and as we talked. Want to hear it? I just have the beginning."

"OK."

"Love is like a cottonwood tree in summer,
It is always cool,
it can never die,
drought cannot touch it,
because its roots
are in underground water."

Livy smiled her old smile, and the wrinkles

in her forehead spread out and disappeared. It seemed like her whole soul rose up and entered into Wilder, and he felt strong and brave again looking at her, still sitting on the couch.

She looked bigger.

"Son, I'm already looking forward to seeing you come back, so I can smell Texas on you."

"I'll be as dirty as Coffee when I get back. You got that right, Momma."

Livy got up, and went into the kitchen but turned as Wilder walked back to his room.

"And Wilder, this cancer is a long way from getting your Momma."

CHAPTER TWO

Leaving

Wilder tried to pack his clothes in his room but kept getting derailed. He just couldn't seem to care about planning a week's worth of necessities. If not watched, he could go a week without brushing his teeth, combing his hair, or showering. Livy kept checking his bag throughout the day and adding all the needful items.

Wilder was careful about his gear, however, which included his hunting stuff and, for this trip, his cowboying gear. Wilder packed his riding boots and spurs, chaps, heavy jacket, vest, leather gloves, black silk neck scarf, and his calf rope. He usually packed books too, but left them out. Papa's house was full of beautiful books.

The Goods didn't own any horses, although Wilder had grown up on them. They were simply too expensive to keep, and their little five-acre lot on the edge of Cottonwood wasn't big enough to keep a horse without its tearing up the ground and turning it into a mudhole. So Wilder didn't have any of his own tack, and he surely didn't have a saddle of his own. Wilder longed for a saddle.

Gale Loving, an elder at the Goods' church and Wilder's adopted "old man" who was sort of a mentor to him, kept a band of saddle and pack horses at his place on the lake, and Wilder rode them all the time using a series of Gale's saddles as he grew. He would rig a different size seat every few years and personalize it in his own way. But he knew they weren't his, and that fact gnawed at Wilder.

He hinted to his parents about a saddle every year at Christmas and his birthday, and they always told him he needed to wait. He was still growing, and it wasn't worth it to buy a saddle. Of course, again, the other reason was money; a quality used saddle started at 500 dollars. Wilder understood that, what he could, but he was still a boy.

Wilder didn't feel poor, as some kids do. He was too busy outdoors, and they were happy as a family. Hank was a carpenter and worked for Gale's construction business when he could, providing money for Livy's care. But that left very little for extras. The one thing Wilder hated, though, was always wearing holey jeans. They were always hand-me-downs from his best friend, Gary Beggs. Gary, who Wilder had always just called Big, was his age but twice his size it seemed. Both knees were always worn out to some degree. Big was bigger, but he was also clumsy. Sometimes Livy patched the knees, which Wilder disliked even more.

The next morning, Wilder would be riding the bus to Texas, Amarillo exactly, where Papa would pick him up. He didn't really like riding the bus, but he knew it was a sign of his independence and trust from his parents. There were lots of weird people on the bus as Wilder saw it. Thinking he was John Wayne—he had watched all those movies over and over—he packed his hunting knife and kept it right at the top of his bag. He had ridden the bus before. Wilder gave up the half-hearted packing and went to sleep.

Hank woke his son in the morning and told him they'd be leaving in 15 minutes for the bus station just as the phone rang. Molly clambered through the house to answer it. After chatting for several minutes, she looked at Wilder with her big brown eyes as he crossed the living room with three cans of Dr Pepper he was casually sneaking from the kitchen.

"Wilder, it's for you."

"Who is it?"

"You know . . . ," and she nodded her head

and opened her eyes real wide and smiled even bigger.

"Ohhh . . . well tell her I am busy. I'm going to Texas in about five minutes."

He said this as he left the room and hoped his careless refusal would have the desired effect. But just down the trailer house hall he heard Molly hang up the phone.

He deposited the cans of DP in his bag and rushed back to the living room.

"You hung up!?"

"You told me to."

"I didn't mean that. Molly!"

"Well, you're rude. That is what you deserve. Sunny likes to talk to me anyway."

Wilder marched over to the phone. Sunny answered on the second ring. She didn't have to play the games that Wilder thought he was supposed to. Boys know nothing of girls—except that they like them and are drawn to them like a bee to a wildflower.

She started talking before he said a word.

"Hey, Wilder. You're going to Texas, huh?"

"Hey, Sunny. Yes, in just a bit. With my Papa. I wish I wasn't."

"Well, I just love Texas. I love the sky best I think. Every night there is a wonderful sunset, and the coyotes sing and then go off on their little parties looking for chickens and rabbits and stuff. I think I'll probably live there one day just to get it out of my system. Maybe I'll do that, work on a big ranch or something."

"I'm going there to work, not play. Papa will have me digging postholes by seven every morning."

"Ha ha, that's great. I wish I was going. You want me to take care of things for you at school?"

"Take care of things?"

"Yeah, get your homework, take notes in class, tell you what you missed. That kind of stuff."

"Sure, I guess so. But I already have some homework for the week."

"OK, I will. You think you'll get to deer hunt and work cattle, too?"

"Yes, probably. Papa said he had some hands coming to brand."

"Ohhh, I am so jealous. What horse are you going to ride? Are you taking your rifle? And take some pictures!"

Wilder interrupted her.

"Sunny, I have to go. Dad started the truck."

"Oh, OK. Have fun, Wilder. Bring some Texas back for me."

He hung up and wished he hadn't. He just couldn't bring himself to be sweet to her, even though he loved her, or thought he did, and would replay every word she had said, searching for hints of affection. It was as if he just didn't know *how* to be nice to her.

Wilder hauled his bags, one with his gear and a backpack with schoolbooks, out to the front porch where Livy waited to hug him goodbye. They didn't say anything to each other. They hugged and cried a bit, and Wilder said, "I love you, Momma."

She slapped him on the rear as he picked up his two bags and turned to the truck.

"You're my baby boy," she said and shined a smile that made him strong again.

ᘉG™

CHAPTER THREE

The Plains

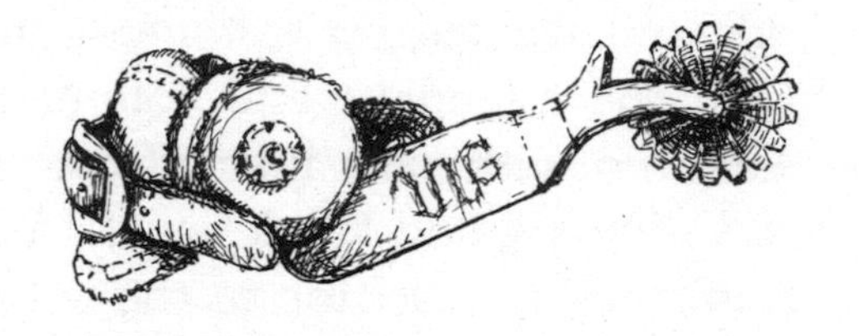

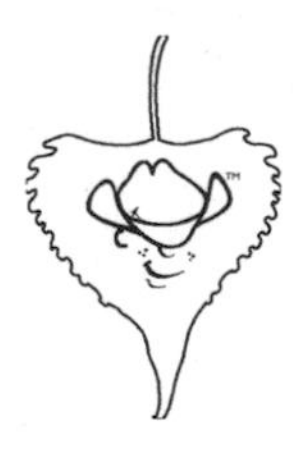

Hank helped his son check in at the bus station. Wilder wouldn't have called it help; he would have called it—standing there and watching him. Wilder carried his two bags inside and walked up to the counter. He spoke with the attendant and bought his ticket to Amarillo with cash his dad had given him. It was nine AM, and Hank bought a cup of coffee from the big machine in the corner, the kind that drops a cup down and shoots a stream of hot, black coffee into it.

He was careful to let Wilder do everything on his own, riding the line between letting the boy feel abandoned and supported. Hank knew the fragility of life and knew he had to prepare Wilder with all the small things.

They sat and waited for the bus.

"Sit up front, next to the driver."

"Yes sir."

That was all they said until the bus pulled into the bay. Wilder stood up and grabbed his bags and walked out to it. It was hard. He had to force himself to go. But he also knew it was what he must do.

Hank followed behind him. He saw his son in worn-out boots and jeans with a hole in one knee—his gray felt cowboy hat scrunched down to where it touched an ear on one side. He wore his favorite shirt, a blue denim pearl snap Wrangler shirt. Wilder's spurs jingled from inside his bag. Hank could feel the tears his son was fighting back.

And he smiled at him, for he was a good, strong son.

"Wilder, it's just like a week of summer camp . . . except that your counselor is a mean old rattlesnake."

Wilder turned around and smiled and looked up at his dad.

"You're right, Dad. No big deal."

"I'm sorry about all this, Bud. It's not the way I drew it up." He paused looking off. "We just have to figure it out, one little bit at a time."

"I know, Dad."

Hank slapped Wilder hard on the shoulder, which counted as a hug between them, and Wilder stepped on to the bus. Hank followed him up and said a few things to the driver, looking serious, making sure he knew that Wilder belonged to somebody.

The bus pulled out of the station and lined out on the interstate heading south to New Mexico and then into Texas. Cottonwood lies at the foot of the Rockies at an altitude of around 6,000 feet. Amarillo was eight hours away on the flat plains at 3,000 feet, which was called the Llano Estacado or Staked Plains. They were named by the Spanish explorers who were the first Europeans to traverse them, 400 years ago. They had been terrified by the flat, featureless plain. Unlike those first explorers', Wilder's trip by bus really wasn't a very long or difficult one, just connecting two dots on a flat page of land with nothing but grass in between.

But that grass was now fenced off into huge ranches, and Wilder loved watching the landscape, watching the ranch country go by mile after mile. In the long stretch between the Raton Pass and Clayton, New Mexico, he saw cowboys moving a herd of Hereford cattle along the fence. They were close to the road, and he strained against the bus window to take them in. He counted four cowboys riding three sorrels and a buckskin. Despite the blacktop road, there wasn't a sign of civilization in any direction. No houses or vehicles or even telephone poles. Just men on horseback.

Wilder's heart raced. All he wanted in the

world was to cowboy. Not to *be* a cowboy—but to do the work, to live the life, *to cowboy*.

As the cowboys passed by and the dust from the cattle's hooves drifted over the road and disappeared into the sky, Wilder rustled in his bag for his spurs. He pulled them out and spun the rowels. Wilder loved his spurs. Something about them, holding them, wearing them, using them horseback—filled Wilder up. Those spurs were his link to the life he wanted.

The pair he held were not expensive custom spurs like professional cowboys owned. These were a cheap pair he had bought at a garage sale. But he had paid for them with his own money, and they were worn and black, and they worked. The rowels were big brass stars that Pancho, at the saddle shop, had swapped out for him. The brass sang when he walked or rode, and that sound was his music.

He had been scratching his brand into the steel on the outer sides of both of them—the same way an expensive set of custom spurs would be silver inlaid. Now he took out his pocket knife and began again. The brand he had thought up for himself was a running "W" with a small "G" attached. Those were his initials but stylized to old brand patterns. His knife couldn't make much of a scratch, and he sometimes cut himself doing this and had to stop to suck the nick dry as a dog will do, which Gale had taught him. But he kept at it, prideful of his work and brand. The work dulled the knife for any other use, but he only used the utility blade in his two-bladed pocket knife. He kept the other "spey" blade sharp.

A little further on, he counted 22 antelope standing and staring at the road. The herd seemed frozen like a museum exhibit, bucks with long black horns and each animal a bright orange with a puffy white rump. Antelope never came anywhere near the mountains, and they stood out like a road sign when you saw them. They stood out and yet they fit perfectly into the composition of the landscape, which made Wilder think of the buffalo.

All the Old West books he read spoke of the buffalo that had once covered these plains. He had a hard time believing that people would shoot them and let them rot, by the thousands. He just couldn't visualize leaving a whole freezer full of meat on the ground. Teddy Roosevelt, among others, had stepped in, realizing that they needed to be saved back then. Teddy had hunted the plains and canyons around Papa's ranch and had been a friend to the great Comanche chief Quanah Parker, and Quanah Parker made Wilder think of Charles

Goodnight. Goodnight was *the* legendary Texan, and his great-grandfather had known him.

Wilder's mind wandered off into daydreams of horses and teepees and cowboys and Indians as the big bus rolled through that great empty space, on the black road twisting like a river. His finger, which had been strumming the star-shaped rowel for thirty minutes, slowed to stop, and he slept, spurs in hand.

CHAPTER FOUR

Papa Milam

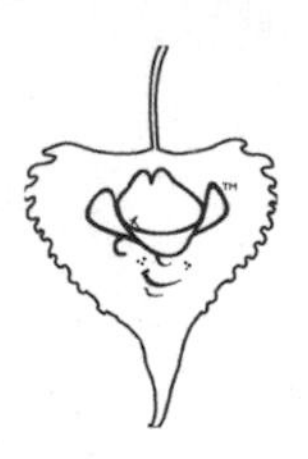

The bus was quiet and sleepy when it drove into Amarillo on time. Wilder looked into the parking lot and knew immediately that Papa Milam was there waiting for him. His rig sat in the lot taking up the entire back row of parking spaces—a grubby, white flatbed pickup and trailer. The truck was a four-door diesel, a Ford, covered in red mud. It wasn't fresh mud on a clean truck from a big splash like a high-school kid would do. It was an old grime that covered the truck, giving it a gray appearance but with two bright, clear places in the front where the wipers cleaned the dirt and bug splatters from the cracked windshield.

A medium-sized dog lay in the shade of the trailer tongue. That was Coffee, Papa's blue heeler. Wilder loved that dog and he always looked forward to sleeping with her at night (something his mom would never have allowed).

Attached to the pickup was a 32-foot gooseneck livestock trailer. The trailer was covered with another substance—green cow manure. The green lines poured down from every side over the rusty white paint of the trailer. The green streaks looked like seaweed; they were mossy, almost pretty from a distance. The "gooseneck" of the trailer reached into the bed of the pickup and attached to a ball there, making for one long, fluid but filthy machine.

Then Wilder smiled when he saw what was in the trailer. Two saddled horses.

The bus parked, and Wilder was standing up with his bags by the time the air brakes released. Wilder nodded to the bus driver and reached out and shook his surprised hand. He said, "Thanks for the ride, sir," with a sincere face but without making eye contact since he was turning out the door as he said it.

Wilder dragged his bags down the three steps to the street, and there was Papa.

"Hello, son," Papa said mildly but with his heart in his throat. He smiled and felt a rush of youth at seeing his only grandson. Young people made Papa feel alive, not tired, like some old people. He was always looking for some kind of action, some excitement. Papa liked other people, especially young people, which was rare among old cowboys and ranchers. Most of them simply preferred to keep to themselves.

"Hi, Papa. How's your grass?" Wilder returned, smiling even bigger but unsure if he was supposed to hug. He didn't want to initiate the hug, anyway.

Wilder gazed at his Papa for a second. He was an old man, at least 75, Wilder figured—although any age over 18 had little meaning to him. Papa was tall and skinny with wispy white hair that blew at the fringes of his gray felt hat—a three-inch brim just like Wilder wore. He was skinny, but solid, and he still walked tall and firm like a young man. He wore his ever-present sunglasses, tinted dark to fight the Texas sun, which he now removed and folded and hung in his shirt pocket. It was a sign of respect to look someone in the eye upon meeting. Out of his dark brown eyes grew deep crow's feet that creased the old man's skin with the look of leather. He was always clean-shaven in the morning, but now in the evening, he had tiny white whiskers sticking out all over that you could have struck a match on.

He had on straight-leg Levi's and a white long-sleeved paper-thin western shirt with pearl snaps. It was torn in three places. The inside collar was dark brown. He wore high-heel riding boots with spurs attached—spurs that never came off. Papa was a cowboy, inside and out. And although he'd visited many places, that's all he had ever really been, or wanted to be—a cowboy.

He was also a widower, Wilder's grandmother having passed several years before. Wilder didn't remember her, and didn't speak of her with Papa, although Livy spoke of her often. Wilder knew that before his grandmother died she and Papa had traveled considerably around the United States, going to national parks; and they had made one trip to Europe. Papa had served in World War II in France and Germany, and they had retraced some of those steps. Wilder liked the photo albums his grandmother had made, and thumbed through them when he had the chance.

But now Papa never went anywhere. He was happy to be at the ranch.

Papa motioned to grab his bags from him, and Wilder handed them over, but he held onto his spurs.

"Grass is fine, could be better," Papa said. His eyes sparkled. "I see you are ready to ride."

"Yes sir, Papa, I'm ready."

"You bring your rifle?"

Wilder smiled. His "rifle" was the .270 that Papa Milam had given him.

"Papa, you can't ride the bus with a gun. I checked. They think I'm just a kid."

"Well, I guess we know better, don't we?"

"Papa. Did you hear I got an elk with it last week?"

"Yes, your momma told me that."

Wilder looked up and searched his grandfather's eyes for approval. The old man smiled down, a wide and honest smile, which was as good as 100 "good jobs."

They broke the eye contact and turned and walked together. As they approached the truck in the parking lot, Coffee stood up on the bed and began to whine and wag her tail. Her ears were straight up like two big triangles that more closely resembled a bat's than a dog's ears.

"All right, Coffee, come and see him," Papa called.

Coffee understood perfectly and exploded from the flatbed of the pickup and ran to Wilder's feet. Wilder dropped to one knee and hugged and scratched the happy dog. She was a heeler with a double mask, which meant her face resembled a coon's, with two black eyes.

They loaded Wilder's bags into the back seat of the truck. Coffee rode in the cab sitting in Wilder's lap with her head out the window.

"You ready for some work, son? I've got a little job to do still."

"Sure, I guess. It's almost dark though."

"That's true, but I've always liked a little night ride."

"Night ride? You mean those horses in the trailer are for us? I figured they were done for the day."

"No, I promised a buddy I would check his river pasture, so I have to. Picking you up put me behind. We just have to ride the bottom a mile and back. He's got some weaners in there, and I need to make sure they're still there. Weaners are jumpy.

"You hungry?" Papa added.

"Yes sir, I'm starving."

Papa was heading east toward the ranch, and after the highway dropped off the caprock into the canyon country and rolling plains where his ranch lay around the tiny pioneer town of Verbena, he pulled into a roadside Allsup's. They went inside and bought Dr Peppers and two fried burritos apiece. The smell of the fried tortillas filled the cab as Wilder ate his like it was candy, burrito in one hand and hot sauce packet in the other. Wilder would load the burrito with sauce and then take that bite, over and over, until the burrito was gone. It was about two sauce packets per burrito. The burritos were lousy by themselves, the sauce worse, but together, when eaten in a bouncing pickup with the windows down and a Dr Pepper between your legs, they combined for a wonderful flavor. The sum was always greater than the parts when it came to Allsup's burritos. Wilder pulled long swigs of DP in between bites. It was cheap food, but to him it was as much a part of the landscape as the sunset that was now falling across their rearview mirror.

The radio played in the background as they ate, and Wilder recognized George Strait singing, "I wouldn't treat a dog the way you treated me-ee-ee . . ." Wilder didn't listen to the radio much, he was never in one place very long, but he knew George Strait's voice, and the cowboy singer Chris LeDoux, and liked them.

Papa always drove everywhere at 45 miles per hour. Wilder didn't know what fast was, since he wasn't a driver yet, but he knew that 45 felt slow. Papa would only drive the highway speed limit if he was driving Grandma's Cadillac, which he still kept in the garage. He called it, and all other cars, "riding cars." A pickup was different. It was a tool just like a tractor or a horse or a wrench.

They left the flat plains of the Llano Estacado, which stop on a jagged line where the entire landscape heading east falls 300 to 800 feet into canyons and rolling plains. All of it for a hundred miles east, north, and south was wild country, inhabited sparsely only by ranches and the people who worked them. Few people ever drove through it, fewer still stopped, and only a trace of humanity lived there. But that's where Papa lived his whole life, and was the second generation of his family to do so.

They drove in the evening light and turned off the pavement to a red dirt road. The mesquites glowed in the soft light, and the red canyon walls seemed alive. Wilder fumbled through his bags in the backseat and put on his gear; chaps, spurs, and riding boots. It was getting chilly and he had no idea where this ride would lead, so he put on his wool vest, too. After winding through the canyon dirt roads for twenty minutes and banging over six cattle guards, they came to a stop in a pasture. Wilder took a deep breath as he pulled the truck door latch open and hopped out. "Here we go," he said to himself under his breath, spurs singing on his heels.

Papa opened the manure-covered trailer door and hollered to the horses to back out, saying "back, back" a few times. The horses weren't tied to the trailer walls. Their reins were wrapped and tied under their necks. They backed up, clumsy, banging their hooves on the wooden floor in the long, empty trailer as they went.

"Papa, I'll grab Fancy, I guess?"

"Yup, she's yours."

Wilder knew he would be riding Fancy since he first saw the buckskin mare at the bus station. But he also knew that when it was time to work with his Papa—and around men in general—you didn't assume anything. You kept an eye on the boss at all times and took his lead for everything. That was how nobody got hurt. That was how you got invited back.

Wilder grabbed the reins that were tied under her neck and pulled the sweet old mare away from the trailer. When he got some space away from Papa, he put his nose to her and smelled her deeply and said out loud but quietly, "Hi Fancy, how are you doing, girl?" as he looked into the gentle horse's big brown eyes.

Wilder walked all around her, running his hands on her coat everywhere he went, feeling and checking her condition and letting her know he was her friend. He checked the bridle and throat latch, the saddle cinch and flank cinch and tightened both a hair, as Papa had them loose for the trailer ride. He led her in a short circle to check that she walked fine and was happy with the way the saddle was sitting. He ended his circle at the door of the pickup where his bag was so he could grab his rope.

Wilder knew there wouldn't be any roping at night, but he tied it onto the horn for the principle of it. A rider without a rope was less able.

He swung up on Fancy's back for a second to check the stirrups and then got off and shortened both of them. It was a full size seat, and when he finally got in it for good, Wilder felt like he was sitting on a large wet log. The saddle was way too big, and the pommel in the front and cantle in the back were so far from his skinny rear and legs that he felt uneasy.

But he didn't say anything, of course, and sat as low as he could, screwing himself down into the saddle to be ready for whatever might happen. The good thing was that he loved and trusted Fancy.

Papa had been up in the seat for a while and sat staring at Wilder, letting him figure it out in what was now almost dark. Papa was riding Bud, a sorrel gelding with a Four Sixes brand he had bought from that famous old ranch that was also in West Texas, but further south.

"Comanche moon tonight, Wilder. It won't get much darker than this."

"Yes sir. What are we doing?"

"There's a bunch of weaning calves in here that I've been checking for Boots. I just need to make sure they are still here. Weaners are liable to be anywhere for a week or two after they get pulled off their mommas. Their mommas are liable to be anywhere, too."

Wilder nodded as they turned and rode, their cow horses stepping out, heads down and quiet, like ranch horses do. Their spurs went "ching, ching" with every step, as the big rowels hung out in space at the end of their boots. Wilder followed Papa a few steps behind as their horses snaked a path through the mesquites and cedars. The mesquite thorns scratched his leather chaps when he came too close to the scraggly trees.

A bunch of coyotes went off, like Sunny had predicted, rallying for the evening's depredations. A bull bat buzzed the two riders, its wings making that primal squawking-roaring sound as it rushed by. The evening air was cool and getting cooler. The moon was peeking over their shoulders to east now, coming up through a cottonwood grove. It was so bright Wilder looked down and saw his shadow on the ground, long and tall and horseback, bouncing to a rhythm. The world seemed as fresh and raw as it must have been at the beginning. That's the way this country was . . . untouched.

"Which makes this night ride a little tricky," Papa continued, although it was several minutes later. "I don't want to pressure anything or make much noise. I just want to see 'em. I don't need a count tonight. Hopefully they'll be at one of two tanks getting a drink, which will make it easy. We'll see them in the moonlight and turn around and come home.

"Plus, like I said, I always enjoy a little night ride."

"Yes sir, Papa. Me, too."

CHAPTER FIVE

Deer Hunt

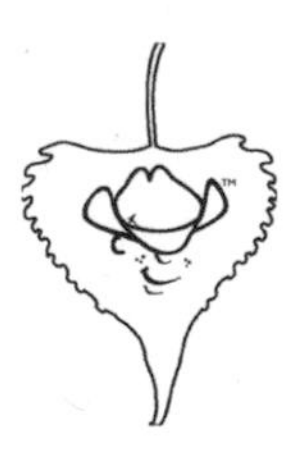

They found the weaners where Papa had said they would be, and then they rode back to the truck and drove to Papa's ranch in the dark. Wilder walked into the ranch house around ten PM after unsaddling the horses and turning them in to the horse trap. He collapsed on the couch, and Coffee immediately curled up on top of him.

Papa left them lying in that same place when he went out the next morning at six AM. He knew that yesterday had been a long day for a 12 year old and decided to allow Wilder the luxury of a sleep-in on his first morning.

Wilder woke up in the strange surroundings and smells of a different house. He had sudden pangs of sadness as he came to, boyishly longing for his home and family and all those accustomed things. He was still in his clothes as he kicked Coffee off his legs and stood up in the strange house.

Sore now, Wilder realized as his body felt

creaky, a sensation he would get used to. Riding a horse employed an entirely fresh set of muscles and joints and ligaments. It took a while to get that hollow between his legs wallowed out, to where the horse and leather saddle fit snug and secure. His stitches tugged at the skin on the back of his calf.

He looked around and saw Papa's houseful of books. It was an old house that smelled old and like books. Papa was a reader and always had been. He had a college degree in Agriculture, but he had minored in English and had long been a lover of books. His book collection spanned all subjects, and Wilder loved walking along the shelves and thumbing through the volumes.

The hundred-year-old house had been added onto every 20 years or so as good calf crops came by, and it sprawled out in all directions, with bookcases lining most of the walls. Deer heads, mule deer and whitetails, were perched in gaps between bookcases in some places, but they were dusty and cobwebbed.

The house smelled like wood smoke. The big main fireplace burned in the living room all winter, and there were two small old-fashioned potbelly stoves elsewhere in the house that Papa sometimes fired up. They all leaked smoke. Papa primarily burned mesquite wood, and sometimes Wilder would catch a whiff of that sweet wood's smell on somebody's backyard grill in Colorado, and his mind would race back to Papa's house. Papa rarely turned on the furnace or air conditioner. The inside temperature of the house usually reflected the outside temperature pretty closely.

Wilder let Coffee out on the front porch and stumbled after her into the bright sunlight. The house sat in a low spot on a rolling plain of improved pasture, spotted with mesquite trees. There were big trees around the house, ancient cottonwoods whose roots sipped the shallow ground water that his great-grandfather had known was just under the surface. Great-grandfather Milam had built the first part of the house in 1912. It was an old ranch, and as such everything was made of wood and was broken in and weathered. The barns, corrals, gates, and sheds were all gray plank boards.

The fall had turned the cottonwood leaves golden yellow, and they flickered and whispered and fell and fluttered down all around the ranch grounds and buildings, which grew up at their feet.

Wilder looked and saw that Papa's truck was gone, but he heard its diesel engine in the distance. He saw his dust in the dirt road behind a bluff covered with shinnery oak a mile away, and soon the truck appeared and came up the drive to the house. Wilder stood looking from the porch, shirt untucked, blue jeans slung low onto his feet, and still wearing socks. His hair was sticking up wildly.

Papa got out of his pickup and came up to the porch.

"Morning," Papa offered. "You look interesting."

"I slept with Coffee on the couch all night. Sorry I didn't get up with you."

"Well, you put in some overtime last night," Papa said. "Let's find something to eat inside."

The cooking was never very complex. Papa hired a woman, Marisol, to do his grocery shopping and bring him food once a week. There were always a pot of pinto beans and stacks of fresh tortillas in the refrigerator. There was always plenty of beef.

They ate together, using tortillas instead of silverware, spooning beans and salsa into their mouths. Marisol had left a strawberry-rhubarb pie, and they both cut off rather large servings.

"You see many snakes this year?" Wilder asked as they ate, always eager to hear about—or kill—a rattlesnake, which was what he meant when he said snakes, which Papa knew as well.

"Not too many, and they're all denned up

already. I only kill them if I catch them up on the porch." Papa replied.

Wilder mused at that answer. "Snakes on the porch?" he thought.

"What are we doing today?"

"Oh, check cattle. We're going to work the calves in the west bodark pasture on Friday. I'd like to get a good count in there, see if they're around."

Wilder felt his insides tighten a bit at the confirmation of a branding on Friday. Checking cows horseback was one thing, but working a branding with his Papa bossing a crew of professional cowboys was another. It was another thing altogether. But Wilder knew how to recognize his fear and still respond calmly.

"How many are supposed to be there?"

"Oh, maybe 80 cows and a few bulls. Don't know how many calves, but I think most of them are done.

"But tonight," Papa continued, "let's go after some fresh meat. Try and get a deer."

That was the sentence Wilder was hoping for. Wilder knew better than to ask for a deer hunt, or to pester an older man, but his heart leapt up when he heard the word "deer."

"That all right with you?" Papa was waiting for the response.

"Yes sir, Papa. I was hoping we could go on a deer hunt."

So they tidied the kitchen as well as they could, and Wilder dressed himself for the day, which meant putting on his hat and boots. When he loaded in the truck he saw a fresh green box about the size of a checkbook on the seat. The box said "Moore Maker" on it. Papa grabbed it and tossed it to Wilder.

"I got you something you'll need."

Wilder knew what it was and carefully opened the unwrapped box. It was the knife he had always wanted, a real Moore Maker, made in West Texas. Wilder lifted it out of the box. Most of the cowboys and farmers and ranchers carried them. This was a fixed-blade knife with about a four-inch blade. It immediately became Wilder's favorite knife.

The handle was dyed yellow cow bone. Into the handle, Papa had the family brand carved—the tree water brand. The brand was a tree forked three ways with a little squiggle line under it representing water. The tree on the brand looked like a turkey track, which was fair, since wild turkeys did roost in those trees every night.

He had heard the story of this brand many

times. His great-grandfather had bought this ranch because of the cottonwood trees he saw growing tall and strong, even though there had been no live water there. It was an old buffalo wallow with shallow and sweet ground water. So he built the house and began buying up land around that main middle pasture that had the cottonwood trees on it. Now the place was nearly 10,000 acres.

In addition, Wilder knew that the brand also had to do with his great-grandfather's love for the King James Psalms. There was a hand-hewn cottonwood board in the house over the fireplace. It was rough and long and looked out of place stretching past the mantle on both sides. Carved into the pulpy grain was, "And he shall be like a tree planted by the rivers of water, that bringeth forth his fruit in his season; his leaf also shall not wither; and whatsoever he doeth shall prosper." This was from old great-grandfather Milam.

Papa himself read the Psalms but had a hard time being tied to churches, or sitting in one, or even one church in particular. But privately he respected the Old Book, and Wilder knew it.

Also in the knife box was a leather holster rigged to hang slanted forward on your belt, so it could be ready in a hurry at a branding or some other cowboy emergency. Plus, Wilder just thought it looked cool. There was a whetstone in the box, too. Papa was forever complaining about a dull knife, saying, "A dull knife is worse than no knife."

Wilder told his Papa thanks and knew not to make a big scene out of the gift, even though it might have been the best thing he had ever been given. He pulled off his belt and put the holstered knife on. He pulled out the blade and thumbed it a bit as they rode, checking how sharp it was. Papa noticed.

They checked cows and drove over about 50 cattle guards it seemed. Wilder was quick to jump out at wire gates and open and close them without being told. Papa waited in the idling truck while the skinny kid struggled with the taut barbed-wire gates. They swung through Verbena and got Wilder a Texas hunting license and a Dr Pepper. They arrived back at the ranch around three and began fussing around for the deer hunt.

Papa pulled his Winchester 30-30 from behind the truck seat. It had open sights and had very little blueing left. It more closely resembled some sort of worn tool in a metal shop than a functioning rifle. On the porch, Papa oiled it down for the hundredth time in his life and handed it to Wilder. Wilder turned away from the old man to point it in a safe direction and ran the lever action, checking it for shells and condition.

"Let's walk to the creek bottom. There's always a mess of deer down there."

"Yes sir. I love hunting down there. Are the deer rutting?"

"I think so. I've seen a buck or two acting silly."

Wilder's heart leapt again. A chance to hunt whitetails with the rut on was as exciting as hunting could get. Every year in late November and early December, the whitetail bucks went crazy trying to breed does. The woods on the creek and river bottoms would be alive.

Soon they were walking through the mesquites towards the cottonwood bottoms of the creek bed. Papa carried his recurve bow, which had been his hunting weapon of choice since Wilder had known him. Wilder walked behind Papa holding the rifle. The sleeves of his camouflage coat hung past his hands and swung back and forth like elephant trunks as they weaved through the mesquite trees on a game trail. About a half mile from the house, Papa stopped and looked into the river drainage.

"It ain't much of a way to hunt, but let's sit in your mother's blind. It's right here close and gives us a quiet entry to the bottom since it's already pretty late."

Wilder nodded, switching into a hunter's instinctive quiet voice. It was three-thirty, which gave them a couple of hours to hunt. The sun was bright and it was unseasonably warm, in the high 60s, which wasn't good for a rutting evening. A warm front could shut down the deer movement, whereas a cold snap always made the deer even crazier.

They found the wood blind that sat on a bluff looking straight into the wide creek basin. The blind was nestled into some fallen cottonwood logs and backed up to cedars behind it. There was a large pile of sticks and forest trash piled up around the rear and one corner of the blind, which was evidence that a pack rat had taken up residence underneath.

Wilder and Papa bent down and walked into the small wooden enclosure and sat down in two chairs that were waiting for them. Wilder leaned the gun, still unloaded, into the corner. The front window was just an open space and provided a good view of the immediate area. Papa handed Wilder three 30-30 shells from his pocket. Taking that as permission to load and make the rifle ready, Wilder grabbed the gun and did so, sliding the three bright brass rounds into the magazine but not chambering one, careful to keep the barrel pointed out the window and not hit the sides of the blind and make noise. With the rifle loaded, they were set.

After almost an hour, Wilder had leaned back in his seat with the chair resting against the back of the blind and his feet up on the front under the window. The rifle was in his lap, pointing out the window. Wilder nodded a bit from the heat in the blind. Papa watched the woods.

Seventy-five yards away in the bottom of the creek bed, Papa caught movement. One doe . . . another doe, trotted out in the open, moving like something was pushing them. Then, immediately after the two does, a white-tail buck appeared with his nose about 18 inches off the ground and a heavy rack decorating his head. It was a massive buck with a swollen neck and every muscle rippling, even under his early winter coat. And he was right in their range. Even though he had killed hundreds of deer, the old man's heart pounded.

Papa wished he was closer and not in a blind, which made his mesquite and bodark recurve useless. He had never gotten over the thrill of the hunt. And having the drop on a mature whitetail buck—there was nothing that compared to it. Mature whitetails were phantoms, wilderness ghosts that were seldom seen up close. The only hope for a deer like that was during the rut, when a true monarch was so distracted chasing does that he forgot all his senses about danger.

And for any hunter, this was the buck of a lifetime.

Papa looked over and nudged the drowsy Wilder, who still leaned back in his chair. But when he did, something caught Papa's eye in the corner of the blind. He refocused and saw it move. It was getting bigger, though slowly. His retinas adjusted to the dim light in the blind—from a hole in the corner and under Wilder's propped up legs, there appeared the triangle head of a diamondback rattlesnake, and it was inching toward them.

CHAPTER SIX

Rattlesnake

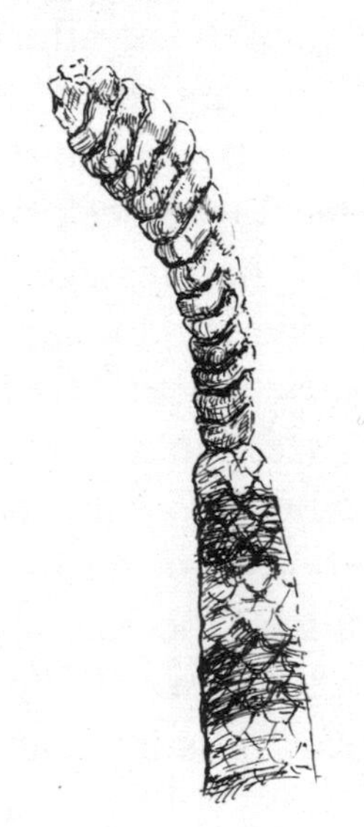

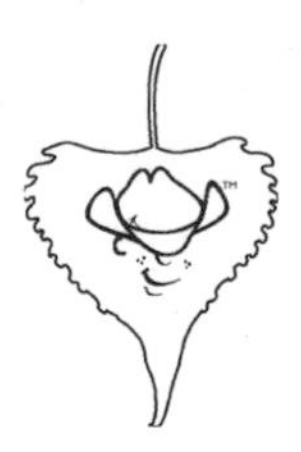

Papa froze. He brought a hand up and placed it on Wilder's chest and mashed down to get his attention. Wilder awoke and looked up into his grandfather's eyes. They were open wide and staring at him from six inches away. He could smell the afternoon coffee on his breath.

"Don't move . . ." Papa mouthed silently and with deliberate slowness. He made a stretched-out head nod, seeking recognition and affirmation of the message.

Wilder nodded, and his heart raced. "There must be a deer!" he thought and, shifting only his gaze, looked out of the blind. He saw the huge buck 75 yards away. He was following the two does around in circles, more or less, as in a trance. The massive rack, which must have been ten to twelve points and spread way past his ears, glistened and shined white in the late day sun. Wilder had never been so close to a mature buck before.

But as his excitement grew, the hand on his chest tightened and shook him, which scared him. He looked at Papa, sheepish, afraid he had done something wrong, though he couldn't think what that might be.

Papa's mouth moved silently again, mouthing the words. "Keep your feet up. There's a snake under you. Pass me the gun."

Wilder's eyes widened to their limits and white showed all around his hazel irises. He sucked in his breath. His heart raced to another level. Papa's hand slid over Wilder's onto the gun.

But he did as he was told. He held his ground. He didn't move a muscle.

Wilder wasn't abnormally scared of snakes, but he wasn't a snake-lover either. He was good at catching them and often did, but he always killed a rattlesnake, every time. But he didn't know whether this was a rattlesnake. He didn't see or hear it—but his mind realized it had to be, to make Papa act kinda spooky and ignore the buck in front of them.

The entire blind was only five feet long and about three feet deep, making a large rectangle box to sit in. The snake was coming through the front corner on Wilder's side, and as Papa looked again, it had about six inches of its scaled body inside—enough to make out four and a half big diamond patterns on its back.

The rattlesnake's big head inched along slowly, like snakes do when they hunt. Its chin just off the blind floor, its black forked tongue worked in and out, in and out, looking for the mice and packrats that it must surely have preyed on many times in this exact spot. Its eyes seemed pure evil, tucked under the eye guards that always slant downward, giving an angry look. The sacks of venom in the cheeks gave the head a triangle shape, as all vipers have. It was an animal designed to intimidate. And with venom packed at the base of its two front fangs like a cow syringe, it was designed to kill.

This was an old and fat diamondback, Papa knew. Diamondbacks were not as naturally aggressive as their cousins that lived on top of the caprock, prairie rattlers. Diamondbacks were bigger and just as poisonous, but they had a calmer disposition, until harassed into a striking defensive position. And that gave Papa his first plan to get out of this mess. Maybe they could wait it out.

Right now, the snake couldn't hurt them, meaning right at that second, and it hadn't sensed them yet with the viper heat sensing "pits" on its face. Only about a third of the way through the hole in the blind, the snake couldn't, and wouldn't, strike at them without the full length of its body to propel it forward. Since Wilder was able to control himself,

Papa thought it best just to watch. He had the rifle gripped hard in his hand now, his hand through the lever, although it still rested across Wilder's lap. He didn't want to shoot inside the blind unless he had to.

The snake had about half of its four-foot body inside the blind now, just about even with the wall in front of Wilder, which meant it was about to be directly beneath Wilder's propped up legs. Papa's mind raced, unsure now of what to do.

Wilder eased a glance down and saw the snake. It was huge. The boy was shocked. He hadn't expected such a fat snake, four inches around at the belly and stretched out for two feet and still coming. The long row of moving diamonds spooked him.

He moved ever so slightly, which made the two chair legs on the ground squeak.

The snake stopped. Its tongue flickered. Its rattle buzzed.

But it was soft buzz, a warning buzz. A primal reaction to a large movement—definitely not a mouse-sized movement.

Wilder's heart raced up another notch. He held his frozen posture and glared up at Papa with wide eyes. His face pleaded for an answer.

The big buck had stopped in the clearing and raised his head to observe a young spike buck approaching the area. He was presenting the perfect broadside shot at 80 yards, but no one saw.

Papa watched the snake. It buzzed its rattle faintly and then stopped, but it started a deliberate action, moving faster. Papa gripped the rifle tight, ready to act.

The snake pulled the rest of its body into the blind, but at the same time retreated and coiled itself into the corner in big looping circles. The big, evil head settled into the middle of the coils to sit and wait and let whatever large animal it had just heard pass, or to snap up the first rodent of the night that scurried through its little trap.

So the situation had gotten better and worse, Papa thought. The snake was settled and away from them, but it was also full ready to strike at them inside the blind. Being about two feet away from Wilder, it was vaguely close enough to strike and hit the boy. It was also getting darker by the second. Tangling with a four-foot snake between them and the door in the dark would be worse . . . much worse.

Papa considered a shot in such close quarters. He knew the slugs would pass through the snake and the old and rotten wood floor of the blind and bury deep into the prairie clay. There was no danger from a close range shot to himself or Wilder, but he thought it through before committing to action.

Then Papa knew what he had to do. The only hitch though, in shooting the snake, was that the gun would have to move considerably, and he would have to chamber a round. Chambering a round on the lever action was somewhat loud and required a lot of movement to bring the lever down to a 90-degree angle and then slam it back up again. That action would almost surely make the snake rise and rattle, maybe even strike.

He would have to be quick. And he could not miss.

Wilder heard the buck snort at his competitor with the two six-inch and crooked spike horns, laughing off, in deer language, the approach of the baby buck.

Papa's hand still on Wilder's chest, he applied some pressure again to get the boy's attention again. Wilder looked up at him, a bit breathless. Papa nodded at his grandson and whispered, "Hold your ears," barely audible as Wilder felt the gun rise off his lap and Papa's eyes switch to the corner. Wilder stopped breathing.

The old man pulled the gun up like an extension of his own arm. As the gun rose the barrel pointed down and the old hands worked the lever action in one blindingly fast movement. The brass slammed into the chamber and the hammer hung back.

Wilder grabbed his ears and closed his eyes and the sound of a mad rattlesnake filled the tiny enclosure. The buzz of a three-inch rattle echoed back and forth in the small, wooden blind.

Wilder wondered what it would feel like to have a snake bite in his thigh.

The model 94's hammer only hung back for a hundredth of a second, for the old man's finger almost instantly released it and sent a slug to the corner of the blind—into the middle of the four-foot rattlesnake.

And then, barely perceptible as a second sound, the hammer fell again as Papa ran the long lever action and fired a second time. The two exploding shots made the deer blind shudder and raised dust from every board, inside and out.

The buck that nobody was watching evaporated into the cottonwoods, bouncing off with his huge white tail waving goodbye.

As the dust and smoke and adrenaline cleared, Wilder felt an immediate sting on his calf, followed by a searing burn.

CHAPTER SEVEN

'Getting pretty western'

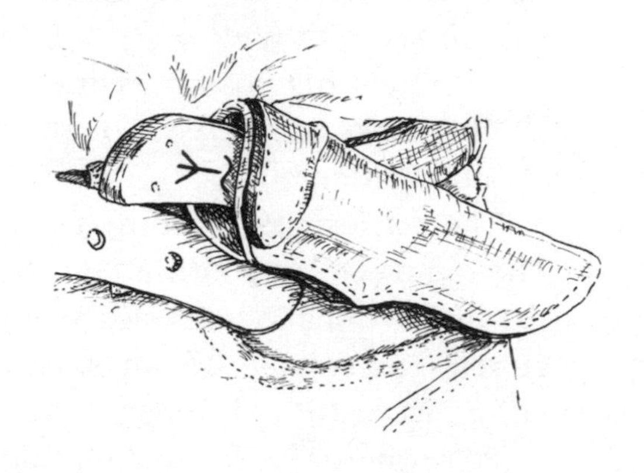

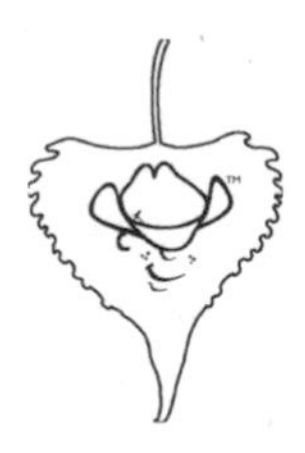

Wilder's frozen posture collapsed with the overload of action. He grabbed at the fire on his calf with both hands as his chair slammed down on the ground. He let out a suppressed "Owww."

Papa held his position with the rifle trained on the snake in the corner, the third and last round chambered.

The rattlesnake was in two pieces, almost. The top piece lay writhing on the ground with the massive snake head still snapping open and closed. The two white fangs, bared and threatening, were an inch long.

Papa knew the snake could no longer strike and so relaxed his aim and moved back to his chair and then looked at Wilder's leg.

"Did he bite you, son?"

"I think so Papa. It burns."

But even as Wilder said that, he felt something in his pants leg. It was one of the discharged 30-30 rounds. It had fallen through the hole at his knee, and the piping hot brass had given him an immediate, although superficial, burn.

"No . . . wait, Papa. It was just an empty," Wilder giggled. "Wow."

"Ha. Wow is right. Good work, son." Papa's eyes were happy and lit. "That was getting pretty western in a hurry."

"That's a big one, huh?"

"Yup, that's about as big as they get . . . Now let's get out of this blind. There'll be no more deer tonight," and Papa nodded toward the door.

They got up, stepped over the dead, writhing snake, and went out the door. They both knew that a dead snake could bite you just the same, if you got too close to the head, but there was no way it could strike since its back was broken.

Wilder knew he would want that big snakeskin and rattle, so he grabbed a stick and went back to the blind and fished the dead rattler out and flopped it on the ground. He stepped on its head with his boot and pulled out the new Moore Maker, which had been riding on his hip all day. He cut the snake's head off and then stabbed it with the knife to pick it up, careful not to touch it. Even the severed head of a rattlesnake was dangerous if you were to fall or mash against it or if a dog found it. So Wilder took it and buried it in the ground about six inches deep, completing the little ceremony that follows every rattlesnake killing. Then he placed a big crumbly caliche rock on top.

Wilder grabbed the snake, smiling and satisfied, and looked up at Papa. The snake moved back and forth, headless and bloody and writhing in his hand, dripping blood from a few places. Wilder acted as if he didn't notice; he couldn't wait to skin it.

"Most snakes are denned up pretty tight by now. That old guy must have come out from the hot weather. He took a lot of mice off this ranch—I hated to kill him."

"Well I didn't hate to kill him, Papa. I was pretty scared."

"There is a give and take to everything out here. It's not a right and wrong . . . but there is a balance."

Papa nodded to himself. He knew a snakebite would have been a mess and he didn't hope for close calls, but that was how it was with snakes and horses and open country. The element of danger seemed necessary to him, and nothing could provide that like wilderness. Talent and experience with those elements made the odds go up, but the risk was always present. Papa relished that, and it was one reason he had remained there so many years.

"That was some buck, too. But I guess we'll have to let him go. You saw him, didn't you?" Papa asked as he turned and started walking toward the house. Wilder followed. The snake was so long it dragged on the ground, which bothered Wilder, but he rearranged it so the headless end dragged and not the beautiful three-inch, coon-tail rattle.

"Yes sir, I saw him. I've never seen one like that before. I wish I could have gotten him."

"Yes, he was a beautiful deer, but I'm kinda glad he got away. I don't think we earned him. I hate sitting in a blind." Papa paused. "How many deer heads can you hang on a wall, anyway?"

Papa thought out loud, "But that blind is good for kids, I guess. I built it 25 years ago for your mother."

"Could you have killed him with your bow?"

"Sure, but it would have taken a lot more work than sitting on your rear with a rifle. A man has to become a part of the landscape to kill with a bow.

"A bow puts in you in company with King David and Quanah Parker. Quanah probably hunted this very ground. Both men knew how to nock an arrow. Technology that is thousands of years old."

They walked through the tall grass pasture. Big clumps of silver-topped big bluestem were all around, backlit by the fading sunset. A nighthawk had starting buzzing them just like the night before. A trio of mourning doves made their sweet fluttering sound as they flew off from the cow tank. Wilder thought about all that bow business. It sounded pretty good, and he said to himself, "I guess I'll have to get a bow now." Wilder heard his grandfather say something out loud but to himself, as he often did, as they got to back to the house, repeating something about being happy the buck got away.

As Papa climbed the steps to the porch and leaned his bow and the unloaded 30-30 against the house, Wilder went into the barn and turned on the lights. He laid the snake out on the shop table and started his cut in the middle of the belly on the headless end. The new knife was sharp, and it unzipped the long snake as Wilder pushed it slowly, inch by inch, along the entire belly.

He stopped around the snake's vent, which gets tricky, and made a few cuts to keep the skin loose when he went to peeling it off. That done, he dug his fingernails in between the snake skin and the meat around the backbone where the head had been. Then he pulled. The large skin peeled off like a tube sock—all the way down until he made the last little cut at the rattle, which left it attached to the hide.

Wilder then went into the house and rummaged around the junk drawers in the kitchen until he found a box of sewing pins. He returned to the barn to find Coffee eating the snake he had thrown on the floor. He took the hide and rinsed it a few times under the water spigot. Before tacking it to the wooden barn wall, he grabbed a bucket and stood up on it to get the snake skin as high up the wall as possible, so nothing could tear it down during the night.

There he tacked the snakeskin with pins, poking them through the hide on the very edges every inch and a half or so. It took him 20 minutes, since the snake was so big and he wanted to make sure it wouldn't shrink too much and pop the pins out and ruin the hide.

It was pitch dark by the time Wilder got back to the house. He scrubbed his hands of snake blood and guts in the sink and walked into the main room where Papa was reading, with his glasses on, like he always was in the evening. Papa's wealth only bought him one extravagance, fine books. Wilder didn't say anything and just stood there, so full of the evening, realizing he had only been there for one full day.

Papa looked up and let the leather-bound volume fall into his lap. Most nights he liked to relax with a good book, but tonight he too was lost in thought and in the happiness of the evening.

"Wilder, I'm glad you are here," the old man mused. Wilder smiled back, unsure and slightly uncomfortable with what seemed like a compliment.

CHAPTER EIGHT

What Ranchers Do

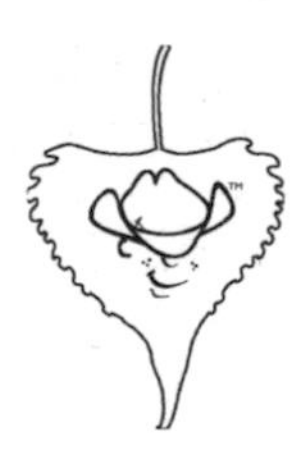

Wilder woke up on the couch again the next morning. He wandered outside in his underwear and socks and stood on the front porch, skinny as a fence post, and watched the sun rise in the east through the front pasture mesquites. As the light peeked through the wiry trees, each paperclip-sized leaf caught the sun's gold and seemed to amplify it. The leaves, hanging off rough black trunks that grew in numerous random directions, appeared to glow in that new morning light.

It was chilly, about 45 degrees, so he didn't stay on the porch long, but he enjoyed the freedom of being outside in his underwear. He wondered what Molly would say.

Papa pulled up in the pickup again and saw Wilder in his underwear and noticed the big white bandage on his calf. Livy had told him about the gash and the stitches but Wilder hadn't mentioned it.

Papa motioned to Wilder's leg, "Those stitches still in there?"

Wilder was pleased it had been noticed, a credit to his toughness. "Yes sir, I guess so."

"Well, you want them out don't you?"

Wilder nodded, his pride turned fearful.

Papa Milam walked past him into the house and motioned for Wilder to follow. He told Wilder to lie down on the kitchen table, which he did in nothing but white socks and white underwear after grabbing a blanket off the couch. Papa rummaged around in the kitchen for his doctoring tools. He put on his glasses and turned on the lights and sat down next to Wilder's bandage. Coffee jumped up on the table and sat down to watch.

"Papa, are you a doctor, too?" Wilder offered, a little shaky, turning his head to see Papa behind him unwrapping his bandage.

"Shoot, I've done more animal doctoring than most vets. But this is nothing."

Wilder turned his head back around and sat his chin on his hands, lying flat on his belly. Papa told him the wound was healed tight and looked good and that he wouldn't even feel it. Papa cut the five stitches with tiny scissors and then pulled the five strings out with tweezers. As if she perfectly understood the procedure,

Coffee began licking the crusty blood along the light red line of the gash.

Papa stood up and said, "Well, get dressed."

Soon Wilder and Papa were in the pickup again, banging around the ranch getting things ready for Friday's branding. They went to town to get propane for the branding fire. They picked up several bottles of vaccine for the calves they would work. They stopped by Marisol's house, and Papa asked her to have an extra big meal ready on Friday afternoon to feed all the cowboys.

Wilder didn't know if he would get to rope on Friday, but he threw about 50 loops every night at a bucket in front of the porch, just in case. Getting to rope at a branding was the highest honor in ranch country, and Wilder made sure Papa saw him practicing. But, like most things, there was no way to learn how to do something and get really good at it except by actually doing it. Roping a bucket and roping a calf horseback were two different things.

One evening while Wilder was roping, a little storm rolled in. They had watched it in the west all afternoon and hoped and wished in silence. It rolled and boiled on the horizon. It didn't have the high, dark blue anvil-top that spring storms have, but it was wet and seemed to be coming their way.

It was a chilly November rain pushed by a cold northern front, and it hit with a big cold air blast—as if somebody had turned on the air conditioning outdoors. The rain ran down the tin roof and made a big line of shimmering water as Wilder and Papa sat on the porch and watched. There is nothing like a rain in dry ranch country. The need for rain was always on everyone's mind, and that need always put everything a bit on edge. Only during a rain did that edge get relaxed, smoothed out to some degree. Everything in the world was right, momentarily, when there was rain on the ranch.

The next morning, Papa and Wilder loaded Fancy and Bud in the trailer and went to check the west bodark pasture where they would be gathering. The pasture was huge and rough, about five sections which made it over 3000 acres under one fence. To save time, they drove their horses to the pasture. Along the narrow ranch roads that connect the ranches and the pastures, Wilder saw an unfamiliar sight . . . another pickup coming.

It was Papa's oldest friend, Red Guffey. He was about Papa's age, but fat and red-haired—although he wasn't all-the-way fat, just his belly. His rear end was tiny, in contrast, and Red always made a big deal out of telling you that he wore the same size pants as he did in high school, which might have been true, only they had to dip way down in front to accommodate the massive belly he had nurtured all the years since then.

The two men had been at school together in Verbena, served in World War II at the same time, although in different places, and then ranched and farmed together their whole lives. They knew everything about one another, and they let each other get away with very little.

As Red approached, each truck slowed and pulled off to the side a bit. The problem was, there wasn't really any "side" to the ranch road. That meant the outside tires on both pickups jumped up a foot onto the pasture level, making the trucks tilt towards the center as they closed the last few feet towards each other. The trucks stopped in the middle of the road, driver's window to driver's window, facing opposite directions. Wilder had to hold on to his door to stay seated and not slide down into Papa.

The two men turned their pickups off at the same time. Papa's window was down already, since it almost never was up anyway.

"Hey, Red," Papa offered.

Red looked in and saw Wilder, and his eyes lit up.

"Howdy, Wendell. Who you got in there? A helper?" Red replied.

"Nah, he's not much of a hand. He just does the cooking. He's scared of cows."

"Is that true, young man?" Red bent down from his window to make eye contact with Wilder sitting in the crooked pickup.

"No sir, that's not true. I am a good hand," Wilder said.

"That's what I thought. Your granddad is a big talker, that's all. I hate to have him on my place. Wrecks everything."

"What have I ever wrecked of yours?" Papa broke in.

That was the opening Red was looking for.

"What have you wrecked of mine?" Red's freckled face and bushy red old-man eyebrows jumped up. "What haven't you wrecked of mine? You drove a feedtruck off the caprock, that's probably the biggest one. You shot my dog."

"I shot your dog on accident, Red. You know that."

"That didn't make much difference to him, did it?"

Red was tickled now. He was winning and doing it in front of Wilder. Wilder sat and watched the two friends tear into each other for five minutes. When they were done, they settled into regular conversation.

"How's your grass?" Papa inquired.

"Holding out, but poor. I fed some cake last week. Did you catch that little shower?"

"Yes, I got two-tenths at the house and thirty-three hundredths on the Upton place. I didn't get nothing over here in the west bodark."

"We'll take it, I guess. I caught a little more, four-tenths, and it came down real fast, and I caught some tank water in a couple pastures. I may sell some cows this winter."

"Rain chances next week. Northern cold front coming in, going to push all this hot air to the gulf for good this year. Supposedly. We ought to see some rain then."

Ranchers always discussed rain in exact measurements. Rain was life. Grass was their product—grass produced beef. Rain was not too far off from religion, consequently. All parts of life in dry country were interwoven, the edges blurred like a rain cloud coming off the caprock, everything and everybody needing the same thing.

Like this, they talked and talked—and Wilder listened—for 30 minutes sitting in their pickups. Eventually, Wilder pulled out his new knife, along with the whetstone that was in his pocket. He held the stone about an inch from his face and spit all over it several times. Then he dragged the blade back and forth, honing the edge as he listened carefully to the men speak.

Once, they both cranked up their pickups, as if they were done, only to turn them off again as they got talking about the Verbena high school football team. Finally, Red asked the last question, which he already knew the answer to, but was asked as a sign of respect to the man who would be in charge of the branding.

"Well, what time you want me there on Friday?"

"Oh," Papa said, acting like it was random and debatable, "usual time I guess . . . sunup. We'll ride over here, take us about 30 minutes, gather, and drive them back."

The trucks parted and each went its way, filled up with the rare conversation in such wide open country.

That afternoon at the ranch, Wilder walked to the tack room in the barn to make sure his rig was ready. He groaned a bit at the thought of riding the huge flat seat that Papa had picked out for him. There were stacks of ropes and reins and old, crusty worn-out saddle blankets all over the room—and 20 or more saddles. There were pack saddles and busted saddles and an old McClellan saddle from the Civil

War era. There was driving gear, hames and harness and collars and leather straps piled and hung and dried out and worthless—a hundred years' worth of leather goods, to try and make use of horse power.

Wilder inspected all of it, fascinated with every bit and bridle and old spur. Sitting on a wooden barrel saddle stand, under layers of harness, he saw a smallish saddle horn peeking out. He wiped the dust off the horn with his hand and saw it bore the ranch brand—the tree water mark—so he dug it out.

It was a medium-sized saddle, about a 14-inch seat, that was well worn and custom made. Wilder could tell it hadn't been ridden in years and was stiff and dry, although the leather was not cracked and ruined like most old saddles get without care. He dusted it off and inspected the saddle closely. It had been ridden plenty in its day. Under the right front fender, he found a small rough inscription burned into the leather. It read "To my Livy."

So Wilder went through the paces to bring the saddle to life, first washing it carefully with saddle soap and then rubbing in neatsfoot oil to every crease and stitch. This job took several hours, but the time went fast as Wilder worked alone in the saddle shed.

Wilder carried the saddle up to the porch

and placed it on the barrel stand, which he also brought from the barn. He sat on it and rocked it around and was immediately thrilled that it fit him perfectly. The high pommel and cantle fit his skinny waist and torso like an old work glove. He adjusted the stirrups which were only one hole too short. Wilder cut up an old inner tube tire and wrapped the horn with it so he would be ready to rope and dally if called upon.

Papa walked up to the porch and looked shocked at the sight.

"Can I ride this old saddle, Papa?" Wilder asked.

Papa's eyes began to water.

Wilder looked at him puzzled and a bit fearful.

"You want me to get off it? I will." Wilder hopped off the saddle.

Papa put his hand out flat and made a gentle pat down gesture signaling to Wilder that he was fine. Then he nodded and croaked a response from his old throat, now tight with some unknown pathos. "It's fine," he said, and went inside the house.

That night, Papa put on his favorite movie, *High Noon*. Wilder had never seen it, but quickly loved it. The theme song by Tex Ritter stuck in Wilder's head—"Do not forsake me, oh my darling," and "If I'm a man I must be brave . . . or lie a coward in my grave." With Coffee next to him, Wilder fell asleep on the couch humming the tune. That night he dreamed he was brave.

Three more days passed with the same routine, checking cattle and fixing little things. One morning, Papa dropped Wilder off in the Upton pasture and showed him the line of postholes that needed to be dug. He left him a water jug and posthole digger and then drove away. He returned four hours later to pick him up. Wilder had wandered some, throwing rocks at prickly pear cactus, but there were fresh blisters on both hands.

Each night, Wilder would drag out his school books. Papa told him he had to do schoolwork each night for an hour and that he didn't want to have to remind him. That was really the only rule that Livy had bothered to tell the old man who would be fathering her son for a week. Wilder half-heartedly did a few math units with fractions and read from his history book about the Civil War. Wilder read the second half of *Beowulf*, which he liked. He especially liked the part about Beowulf refusing to fight with weapons and then tearing off Grendel's arm with his bare hands, which Sunny had told him was disgusting.

Papa didn't mention the saddle, and seemed more aloof as the week continued. He had gathered and worked and branded thousands of cattle, but a branding was still a big operation. It was dangerous work where anyone might get hurt bad. And it was also the very pride of a cowboy—to complete the work properly. Or maybe he was just thinking about Livy, his only daughter.

The last night before the branding, Wilder was on the front porch all evening working on his hat. Papa had been letting him do as he pleased as far as staying up, as long as he was ready each morning, and of course he had been. But tonight Papa wanted him to go to sleep in a real bed and to do it early, so he went out to get him.

Papa walked out to the porch where he found Wilder grinning at his gray felt hat in his hands, admiring it.

"You like it Papa?" he asked the old man, looking up with hopeful eyes. He had made a hatband from the now dried and cured diamondback snakeskin they had killed at the blind days before. The long rattle was rigged so that it kind of stuck out and dangled right in the middle, hanging over the front brim. The hat also had a series of fishing flies hooked into the hatband from his fly-fishing trips with Gale; elk hair caddis, pheasant tail bead heads, and a grasshopper.

But Wilder thought the snake band was the coolest thing he had ever done, and he was eager for the old man's approval.

"Hmmm. Don't be a nester, Wilder," Papa said, crushing Wilder's ambition. "It's time to go to bed."

"What's a nester?"

"A nester is a dude. You don't want to be either. A working cowboy wouldn't be caught dead in anything snakeskin—hats or boots or belts."

"Oh." Wilder replied, wide-eyed and puzzled, but following his granddad inside.

Before he lay down to sleep in bed for the first time in a week, he took the snakeskin hatband off his cowboy hat, stretched it back out and hung it on the wall in the room. Then he laid the hat upside down like always, to protect the special brim crease he had labored to get just right.

ᘎᘎG™

CHAPTER NINE

Gather

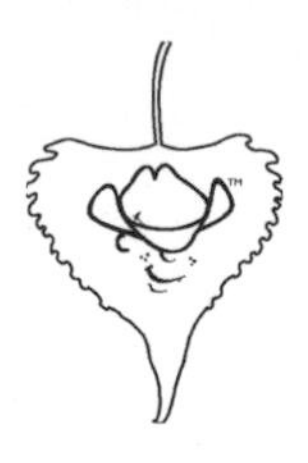

Wilder had a knack for waking up exactly when he told himself to. All he had to do was tell himself out loud, "five-thirty," and he would almost always be able to hit that time. Even he thought it was strange, but it worked. So he arose the next morning in the dark and stumbled to the kitchen where he found Papa drinking coffee and listening to the radio at the kitchen table, shrouded in light from one table lamp. Steam boiled over the edge of his cup. He was staring out the big back window into the dark. As always, the radio was tuned to the public frequency that ran through local, state, and national news and gave the weather report every fifteen minutes. A slight cold front had blown in. It was 45 degrees but was supposed to get colder as the day drew on.

As Wilder pulled up a seat at the table, Coffee jumped up on the tabletop and whimpered at Papa. Without looking at her, his hand found his coffee cup and pushed it to her. The blue heeler drank down the hot coffee in big dog licks and slurps, making a mess. Papa looked over at Wilder staring at the show.

"Kinda funny, ain't it?"

Wilder nodded wide-eyed, his lips making a quizzical crease to one side.

Wilder wolfed down carne guisada, tortillas, and milk. Marisol had sent fresh biscuits too, and Papa had a jar of sandhill plum jelly open on the table. Wilder greedily spooned the reddish jelly onto a biscuit. Sandhill plum bushes grew all over the ranch, and the family had been picking the plums and making jelly since they had been on the place. With Grandma now gone, Papa still picked the spring fruit and delivered bushels of them to Marisol for jelly-making. It was sweet and sour and Wilder's favorite jelly since he was little.

Wilder loaded up a second biscuit and ate it as he and Papa left the house and walked in the pitch dark to the barn. He wore his chaps, black silk scarf, and wool vest. His spurs and the new knife had been permanent fixtures since he arrived. The horses were up in the trap and came running when Wilder rattled the feed bucket. Catching horses in the dark was tricky, even gentle horses. They acted like colts, fighting over position and rushing through gates all at once. The cold made them edgy about everything.

Wilder had to corner Fancy before he could approach her, but when she knew she was beaten, she relaxed and let the boy approach. He eased the reins over her back and caught her under her neck while he slipped the bit in her warm mouth and the leather bridle over her ears.

As he and Papa were saddling, the first light peeked up into the stars to the east. Wilder smoothed and rubbed Fancy's coat and carefully laid his blankets on her. He threw the old saddle he had found on her back and tightened down the cinch and buckled the flank cinch loosely. Papa watched all this out of the corner of his eye as he saddled Atticus, a gray gelding, his favorite roping horse. Fancy stomped around a little more than usual, and Papa noticed.

"Wilder, you might want to warm her up a bit. There's time."

Wilder knew this meant to do it—Papa always said things in a way that gave a person the dignity of making it seem like it was their choice. Wilder nodded and, after walking her in a little circle and away from the barn, grabbed the reins and a bit of mane and legged over.

As he settled into the seat and tried to find the off stirrup, he hit Fancy with that spur a little funny on that left side—a little too funny for a cold morning. The mare wasn't a bucker, never had been, but she took three big crow hops in the dark, and Wilder never had a chance to get balanced. On the second landing, he knew he was off and had to let go.

He crashed in a pile on the buffalo grass in the hazy light of morning. He landed a little on his side, and it knocked the wind out of him. Fancy stopped and stared a few feet away, embarrassed at what she had done, maybe surprised, it seemed. The reins hung down to the ground, waiting for Wilder to grab them again.

Papa heard it and looked and saw the boy plop onto the ground like a sack of cow cake, but Papa stayed put. Wilder rolled over and looked up at the fading stars. There were a few left. The ranch was still quiet.

Wilder gasped for air and knew no one was coming for him. He was mad about that for a second, mad at Papa, as he lay there and thought of how his mother would be helping him out right now, checking him for injuries.

But after five long seconds of lying there, he knew he had to get up. So he did. He rose to a knee and then both feet and took a few hobbled steps while his lungs readjusted to full capacity. His hat had stayed on. He spit twice, dirty, and grabbed Fancy's reins. The old mare looked penitent, and he knew better than to take his anger or embarrassment out on an animal. He patted her on the neck. There was nothing for it but to jump back on, but he paused.

Papa mounted Atticus and walked the big gray gelding over to him.

Looking down at his grandson, he said, "Wilder, you're a little scared right now, that's smart. This is a dangerous business. But it's as simple, and as complicated, as this—you just have to ride through it."

Wilder stared down at the ground for a moment. He tasted the coppery hint of blood somewhere in the back of his throat, perhaps from the impact to his lungs and nose. He heard the rumble of a diesel engine and the rattle of stock trailers banging metal on metal as they were pulled over ranch roads, and he knew the crew was about to arrive. He swallowed, and felt the swallow go down and fall into a big empty spot in his belly, which made him feel a little sick.

Then he looked up at his Papa with a little anger in his eye. "I'll be right behind you . . . you old rattlesnake."

Wilder didn't watch for a reaction as he wiped his runny nose on his sleeve, leaving a long wet streak, and planted a leather boot in the stirrup and swung up into the saddle. He wiggled to balance himself and sat low in the middle—toes up and heels down.

Papa was taken aback . . . the comment hitting him in the face like a leather work glove. Then he broke out laughing in the silence between them.

"Ha, your mother told you to call me that, didn't she?" Papa suspected as he chuckled.

"No sir. But I've heard her say it a time or two," Wilder answered without looking up, waiting for Fancy to try something else on this frisky morning.

"Well, son . . . that is just fine." Papa smiled and stood there mounted, next to his grandson. He was pleased.

Two sets of truck lights sailed up the road and swept past them near the working pens and stopped. The first truck carried Red and his hand Artemio. Artemio had worked for Red for a long time, and the two were usually seen together, working or not. Artemio was from old Mexico and had an exceptional set of cowboy skills, especially with his rope, which he called a *soga*.

In the other truck were a couple of local men who Papa hired for cow work, professional cowboys—Mark and Cotton. They were both married, in their 40s, and cowboyed for various ranches and dayworked some, as well as keeping their own cows.

Papa rode over to their trucks and made

small talk while they unloaded their horses, which were saddled already and riding loose in their gooseneck trailers.

It was an experienced crew, and there weren't any big speeches to be made. When everybody was mounted and ready, Papa pointed Atticus toward the west bodark and they moved off at a walk. Papa had the gates set open in the working pens for when they returned in a couple hours with the herd of cattle.

Wilder had nodded and shaken hands from horseback with everyone. He didn't really know anybody but Red, but that didn't matter. They all knew that Papa didn't babysit anybody, so they were expected to treat Wilder as a grown man, as any other professional cowboy. Wilder knew this too, and relished it. But he also knew he was the rookie in the bunch, with a lot to learn and a hard day ahead of him.

Only Red commented on the grass stain on Wilder's back as they rode across the pasture.

"Wilder, did you sleep out on the range last night, watching the herd?"

"No sir."

Everyone knew what the deal was, for cowboys notice everything about their work and the men they work with. Getting bucked off, or rather, hearing of someone else getting bucked off, was a sublime delicacy. Teasing was a way to welcome Wilder into the group, not embarrass him.

"Well, you really need to do a better job of washing your clothes, being all the way down here away from your sweet momma."

"Mr. Guffy, you know I fell off," Wilder said. "Fancy was a little frisky first thing."

"Oh," Red acted surprised. "Well, that will happen, won't it? I saw your Papa get bucked off an old brindle mule one time . . ."

This started Red off on storytelling as they walked along in two sets of three riders in the thin early light. Most of Red's stories had a way of running down Artemio or Papa or their cows or horses or dogs. His big belly rocked along as he talked, always coming perilously close to the rubber-wrapped saddle horn, which made Wilder giggle to himself.

Wilder spurred Fancy up to the first wire gate to make it clear that he knew his place at gate opening, which meant it was always his job to get off his horse, when getting off a horse was necessary. This particular gate had a good deal of thick mesquite brush grown up around it on the fence line, and as Fancy came up to it in a trot and Wilder loosened his off leg from that stirrup to swing down in a hurry, a hidden covey of bobwhite quail exploded from the brush at the base of the gate. Fifteen fat little birds blew off like oversized bumblebees in every direction, making their dramatic flushing sound. The barbed-wire fence and mesquite brush had been their cover for a night's sleep.

When the quail blew out, Fancy jumped sideways five feet in the same instant. Wilder's hat fell off, but one hand still held the reins and had caught the saddle horn, although his entire body was on the right side of the horse now, dangling there with one foot in the stirrup. Wilder was fine, and Fancy stopped moving, but he did not want to touch the ground, even though he had to get down anyway. So he wrenched himself back up and threw his leg back over the saddle and settled his seat. He patted Fancy, saying, "Good girl."

Without looking at anyone for approval, he walked the horse back to the gate, faking coolness as his heart fluttered, and then dismounted and opened the gate. He grabbed his gray felt hat and screwed it down tight, and then he opened the gate.

Red caught Papa's eye and winked. Papa smiled back.

The men walked and trotted their horses a bit for 30 minutes and covered the three and a half miles through the west pasture to the west bodark pasture. Fancy had lined out and was the smooth, experienced ranch horse she always had been. Wilder's confidence was strong again by the time the sun was shining. The new choice of saddle made a big difference.

Now in the west bodark pasture, the men all stopped and dismounted in silence. They all tightened their front cinches and took a notch out of their flank cinches, as the work turned serious. Then they each got back in the saddle and began to fan out without instruction.

The sun was up, and the clean, cool air was wonderful. They were in a rough and broken piece of range filled with canyons and gullies and mesquite and cedar. It required a thorough check to grab all the cows. There was a windmill and dirt tank a few hundred yards from the gate where they came in, which was where they would meet up, each with his bunch of cattle, before driving the entire herd back to the headquarters and working pens.

Wilder stayed with Papa, watching him closely. He fanned out to his right about 200 yards, which enabled him to see country Papa couldn't, but was also not exactly like the other men. If Wilder got into a wreck some way, Papa wanted know the general area he was in.

It was a large pasture, about 3000 acres, which is nearly five sections, a section being a square mile or 640 acres. The general idea was to ride to the back side of it, taking note of any cattle they saw, and then sweep them all up on their return through.

Papa and Wilder passed two bunches of the Black Angus and crossbred bald-faced cattle as they rode. Papa always made a count. Wilder did too, but he wasn't very good at it. Counting moving cattle was a skill, one of the small arts that made up the cowboy trade.

They reached the back of the pasture in 30 minutes. Wilder had walked his horse all morning, only trotting her to go up hills and embankments, which she wanted to do naturally anyway. As they turned around and rode back, he saw that Red and Artemio had gathered a bunch and were pushing them along the east fence. He didn't see Mark or Cotton.

Wilder and Papa picked up their two bunches of cattle and pointed them towards the gate. They both rode in flank positions behind the cows, both pushing from behind and steering the herd a bit. The oldest rule is that the only way to move cattle fast, is slow, and Wilder knew the rule. Everything was slow and easy. Wilder loved being in contact with the cattle, using his horse as a tool, but more than that, as a partner.

Clearing a pasture big enough for each rider to disappear from all the others and then watching as they all began to reappear, at a distance, with their little bunches of cattle, was a beautiful and satisfying occurrence—each man depending and waiting and watching out for the others at the same time. It was a bare self-sufficiency without being isolated. Cow work was why a cowboy chose the profession—the land, the animals, and the men.

Mark and Cotton appeared pushing a pair of bulls. Sometimes bulls followed right along and sometimes they fought every step of the way, which was what these two were doing. They rumbled and smashed heads in powerful but seemingly slow-motion maneuvers. It was comical from a distance, but Mark and Cotton kept theirs, staying 20 yards behind the bulls to avoid any sudden charges that could easily have knocked them and their horses over and caused serious injuries.

They all met at the water tank and let the cows drink. The riders sat still, in a big half circle about 50 yards back from the cows around the creaking and pumping windmill. The bulls separated and sniffed up some cows and seemed bored with their fight for now. Papa made a count, and he seemed satisfied that they were all there.

After five minutes, the cows started moving off the water, which was the cue to push them to the working pens at the house. Every man had been watching for this and for a subtle move from Papa, which would signal the last leg of the gather. Papa stepped up Atticus and applied a little pressure on the cattle, everyone else did likewise, and the herd began to move to the gate.

When the cattle were all moving again, Wilder rode up behind Papa and took his position at the rear of the herd. He would ride drag, which was the least crucial position for breakaways. It wasn't that Wilder couldn't ride any other positions, but it was part of the code that the youngest man always be ready and willing to take the lowest ranking job. This was never resented.

They pushed the herd, which was a good sized bunch—80 mama cows, 3 bulls, and 70 or so calves—the rest of the way to the pens. Papa rode through the cows often; they were used to horses and men, and that made them easy to handle. Not all cows were like that.

At the pens, Wilder jumped off his horse again to close the gate and trap the cows. The quiet morning of the gather was over, and the loud and fast action of the branding was about to begin.

CHAPTER TEN

Branding

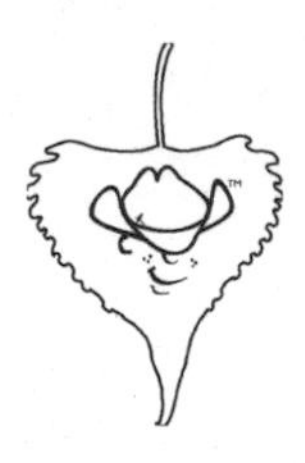

The working pens were made of rough-cut wood planks and had sprawled out in every direction since the first posts were laid in the early years of the ranch. Cottonwood trees lined most of the fence rows and alleyways. The cattle were in the first large pen, called the "grass trap," which was about the size of two football fields. The first job was to cut the cattle, which meant to separate the cows from the calves so they could be worked by the men.

Papa and Red rode into the herd as Wilder and the rest of the men fanned out in the pen cutting it into halves. Papa gave Atticus a loose rein and let him move among the cattle and start picking off the mama cows and bulls, separating them from the calves. Red and Papa watched their herd, and their horses did too, with lowered heads and pinned ears, sending back groups of three and four cows to the other end of the pen, past the other riders and into another catch pen. Red and Papa were old hands at cutting, and their horses were, too. With light pressure on the herd, the cows seemed to cut themselves naturally.

Papa was gentle on his cows. Men who were rough on them, or hotheaded, only worked with Papa once.

Wilder sat on Fancy at the back of the pen and studied everything, ready for a chance to do something, but knowing that his job, first of all, was to stay out of the way.

Soon the cows and bulls were cut out of the herd and penned away from the calves in a large, adjoining holding pen. The remaining 70-plus calves looked cold and lonely huddled together, and they began bawling back and forth with their mothers. They were driven into the next pen, a smaller one where the branding work would take place.

The six riders dismounted in near-silent unison, loosened their cinches a touch, and tied their horses loosely in a row on the fence line outside this pen. Then everyone went to work setting up the branding tools; Papa went for his vaccine equipment, Red grabbed a big orange water cooler, Mark and Cotton picked up the propane bottle, branding iron heater, and branding irons from the front of the barn where Papa had placed them, and Artemio assembled the other tools—a dehorner, a feed tub to hold tools and ear notches, and some mesquite chunks for the heater.

Wilder didn't see anything to do, so he pulled out his whetstone, spit on it, and began fine-tuning his blade to be sure it was ready if needed.

The propane burner was soon roaring, and when Papa was sure the irons were hot enough for work, he nodded to Wilder, "Why don't you rope a few with me."

Wilder's heart stopped. He gulped in shock and felt his hands get shaky.

"Yes sir," the boy nodded back and started for his horse.

He had never roped with Papa before, but now through some invisible graduation ceremony, he had been promoted and was going on to the next level of his education.

Papa and Wilder tightened their cinches and, for the first time that day, took the slack out of the flank cinches. They pulled these just tight enough to make contact with the horse's belly, so their saddles would stay tight when the weight of the calves pulled against the saddle horn, which would anchor their ropes.

Papa always kept the calves in the end of the pen closest to the mama cows. This was so the silly and confused calves would always be facing their bawling mamas, leaving their rear legs exposed for easier heel catches with a rope.

Papa built a loop, eased up to the herd on his gray gelding, made one circle over his head, and dropped a perfect heel trap on a calf. As the calf stepped up, Papa jerked the loop tight and made a dally around his horn. Then Atticus turned without being told and headed to the fire with a double-hock catch.

"He sure makes that looks simple," Wilder thought, as he moved up to the calves, taking the place which Papa had vacated. His loop was built and hanging by his side in his right hand. There were 70 pairs of legs to choose from, but he centered on one, twirled his loop once over his head, and threw his trap. The grayish-white calf rope fell perfectly and skipped under the calf's belly. The loop wrapped itself around the two hocks, causing the calf to jump forward and right into the open trap. Wilder pulled the slack high in the air, felt it tighten, turned, and wrapped a dally around his saddle horn.

He was both shocked and elated. He had a double-hock catch on his first attempt! He wanted to yell out, "Did you see that!!!" . . . but he knew better. He spurred Fancy lightly to the fire. Papa glanced up while coiling his rope and unconsciously made a surprised look.

Mark and Cotton, being the youngest of the

men, had taken the first positions on the ground crew running the rope. When Wilder pulled his calf up to them, one man stood on either side. Mark grabbed the rope that was stretched tight between saddle horn and the dragging calf's hocks; Cotton grabbed the calf's tail. Without a word, in one perfectly synchronized movement, Mark pulled the rope high in the air while Cotton pulled the calf's tail low to the ground. The calf made a tremendous spin in the air and slammed down onto the ground on its side.

Mark immediately hit the ground, too. While easing his hands down the rope and onto the calf's feet, he placed his left boot behind the calf's leg that was now lying parallel to the ground, loosened the rope, and held the top leg back, stretching the calf wide open.

Cotton, the tail man, moved on to the front half of the calf in the same moment, placing his weight on the calf's body and pulling its front, top leg up to where it rested between his own legs, holding it bent and tight up against his belly. The calf was now free of the rope but totally immobilized by the two cowboys.

Mark shouted, "Bull calf!" He did this since he had the best view of the calf's sex and to signal that it needed to be castrated.

Red stepped in immediately and bent down

to castrate the calf. He found the furry little scrotum, about the size of a golf ball, and cut the bottom half off. He then placed his knife between his teeth and held it there by the handle while he manipulated the testicles out of the open hole in the scrotum. The testicles were two long, translucent white organs that peeked out at the first cut, but then had to be situated just right and pulled out to be removed properly.

When Red had the testicles out and hanging by the various tubes that connected them to the calf, he took the knife from his mouth and sawed the connection side to side, instead of making a clean slice. The calf bawled, but the rough cut was better for the calf, since it allowed for quicker clotting and healing.

Red got to his feet and threw the scrotum into the feed tub so a good count of the bull calves could be made. He then placed the two testicles on the branding iron heater top, which made a perfect skillet. They fried and sizzled at touching the hot steel.

While Red was doing this, Artemio had already given the calf two shots with the vaccine guns, under the opened armpit of the calf's front leg held up by Mark. Now he was ready behind the calf with a hot iron. He lowered the brand firmly but not hard. The calf's hair flamed up and billows of smoke blurred the whole operation. Wilder caught that smell of burned hair and hide from where he watched, as he coiled up his now loose rope, and he loved it. Artemio held the tree water brand on the calf for about three seconds, wallowing it all around to make sure its imprint left an even mark.

Red had moved to the front of the calf and pulled its right ear up from the ground. He made a swallowtail ear notch, which made the tip of the ear look like a "V." This marked the calf so that from the right side, which is where most cowboys roped, they could tell it had already been branded.

Mark and Cotton nodded at each other, and Cotton shouted, "Clear." Cotton released his hold on the front half of the calf and stood up. Mark, still seated on the ground, transferred his grip from the top leg of the calf to the tail. The freed calf quickly stood up to get away. Mark held on to the tail and was steadily raised to his feet by the retreating calf, which was then released to rejoin the herd, if slightly altered.

The whole process took about a minute, usually, and was fast and tiring work. This was especially true when Papa was roping, for he seldom missed a loop, and the steady stream of bawling calves being dragged backwards never stopped.

Wilder headed back for another calf and thought to himself, "I'm one for one. I might just go a hundred percent today."

To Wilder's surprise, he caught his next calf on his first toss too, if only by one leg, which was fine, and dragged it to the fire. But that was to be his last catch of the day. He swung loop after loop, waiting behind Papa each time, only to come up empty. He began pressuring the calves too hard and chased them a bit and made desperation throws with little chance of success. He wanted to quit. It seemed like it was impossible to rope a calf now. He began to feel that everyone was laughing at him, as they stood at the end of the pen watching his loop hit the dirt time after time. But they weren't. They had all been in his boots, and they all knew it was the only way to learn.

After Papa had roped about half the calves, a mix of bulls and heifers, he nodded at Wilder to follow him to the fence and dismount.

"Red, you can rope a few if you want," Papa hollered over the roaring propane burner and bawling cattle.

Wilder loosened both cinches on Fancy and patted the now sweaty horse on the neck. "Thanks, girl," he whispered to her.

He then walked over to the branding iron heater and grabbed a half-burnt calf fry. He juggled it back and forth between his hands while it cooled. Then he popped it into his mouth, crunched down, and bit the calf fry in half. It was earthy and hot, and made everything settle into a complete morning. He didn't eat them at any other time, but on a chilly branding morning, they were perfect. The hot protein felt good in his stomach, and he ate another as Red readied his horse.

"Wilder, why don't you run the rope for a while."

Wilder nodded at Papa and took his place across from Cotton as Mark stepped back. The calves weighed anywhere from 200 to 350 pounds. They were Angus and Angus-crossbred cattle, which were notorious kickers. These calves fought you, and they were big and strong. Wilder only weighed 120 pounds, and he wasn't sure if he could even hold back a calf's leg.

Red brought a calf in no time, slipping the rope easily between his big belly and the saddle horn to make a dally. Wilder swallowed hard and stepped up to grab the rope. His timing was bit off from Cotton's, but Cotton was a big, powerful man, and his tail jerk slammed the calf down, nearly pulling Wilder down along with it. Wilder slipped into position and soon had the leg stretched back tight. It was a heifer calf, so Wilder stayed quiet.

Papa appeared with the two vaccine guns and jammed one into the calf's loose armpit flesh between the skin and muscle. The calf jerked and Wilder's grasp wasn't as sure as he had thought. The calf leg shot out of his hand-hold and slammed into Papa's arm that held the second vaccine gun.

The needle of the gun lurched forward and stuck right into Papa's other hand . . . and delivered a dose.

CHAPTER ELEVEN
'I like a ready man'

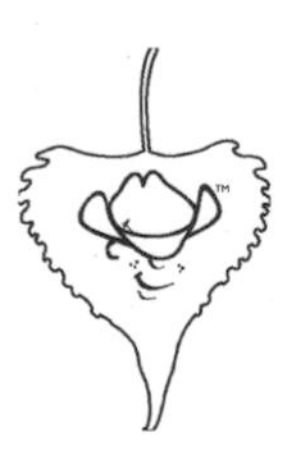

Wilder lunged forward to regain control of the leg. He grabbed it with both hands and stretched it back into position. His eyes were wide, and he stared at Papa, expecting some words.

Papa looked down at his hand. The large cow needle had punctured the stretched skin between his thumb and index finger. As he looked closer, he saw that it had actually gone all the way through the fold of skin and the vaccine dose had missed him as it squirted out the other side. But the needle had skewered Papa's hand through the thick muscle between those fingers, and the big cow needle was about the size of a six-penny nail. Without wincing, the old man pulled out the needle, still connected to the gun. Two little dots of blood appeared and ran down both sides of the hardened hand.

Papa looked down and glared at Wilder. His eyes were calm, but angry. The message was delivered. Wilder nodded. He had better not let that happen again.

Everyone finished working the calf, and Wilder eased up to his feet holding its tail. Papa ignored the wound on his hand.

"Well, Wendell, you won't get pneumonia this winter," Red said, laughing as he walked his horse back to the calves, shaking out a fresh loop.

Papa, Artemio, Mark, Cotton, and Wilder watched as Red caught the next calf by only one leg. When Red saw the rope tighten on just one hock, he let it fall slack so the calf could step out of it. Red and Papa did this often. From the time they were young men, roping had been their pride, and they wanted double-hock catches every time. They might say it was for the ground crew, because it was much easier to flank a double-hocked calf, but more than that, it was a deep pride they had in their job. A cowboy was a working man, a tradesman, and his value was tied to the quality of his work.

Red caught the next one by both hocks, but it was a big bull calf. The bald face Angus cross let out a deep, mature bawl as Red dragged it to the crew. It also had a particularly messy and large amount of fresh, green manure trailing from its rear, all over its tail, and covering both legs. Artemio stepped up next to Wilder.

"Wilder, I can take this one, eh? *Es grande boss.*"

Wilder knew he should let Artemio flank and hold an animal of that size. The boy's eyes checked Papa, who just stared forward at the coming calf. He had only a second to make up his mind.

"Thanks, Artemio, but I think I can get him," Wilder said, as he stepped up into position across from Cotton.

As Red dragged the calf between them, Wilder reached down and grabbed the rope. They didn't have to flank him very hard, as Cotton quickly jerked the calf down to the ground by its tail. The big calf had nowhere to go with both rear hocks caught.

Wilder grabbed the top rear leg, his hand now coated with slick manure, and slid the rope off. He pulled the leg to his belly. He gripped the slimy, green leg with both hands, but it felt like he was trying to hold the fat end of a baseball bat covered in butter. He shouted, "Bull calf!"

Papa came up and knelt on the ground with both knees at the calf's groin and made the cut on the scrotum. Artemio appeared on the opposite side and slapped down the brand. As the brand sizzled and the smoke filled the area, blinding everyone for a second, the big calf bawled and tensed and pulled against the crew.

Once again, despite Wilder's best squeeze on the leg, it popped out of his hands like a pinched watermelon seed. The calf was just too big, the leg too slippery. And there was only one place for it to go.

The heavy leg crashed into Papa—right into his face. It knocked his hat off and caught him on the cheek. It hit him hard and smeared green cow manure from his shoulder to his ear.

Wilder lurched forward to grab the leg, but this bigger calf was already kicking back, and the sharp hoof was loaded for him. It caught Wilder in his perfectly positioned face, sending his hat flying, and giving him a cut under his left eye.

Still, the boy grabbed wildly for the leg with both arms, trying to regain control. As he corralled the leg, Wilder's arms and chest absorbed numerous kicks, and the runny green manure splashed and smeared, decorating the scene.

The other men didn't see exactly what was happening, as the branding iron smoke hid the rear of the calf for the few quick seconds it took to transpire. As the smoke dissipated, they saw Wilder hugging the rear leg of the calf with his body bent forward in a very awkward way. Papa was glaring at him, without a cutting knife in his hand. Both were hatless, covered in blood and dirt and manure.

Wilder stared at the ground as he lay bent over, hugging the calf's leg with all his might. He had let two calves get loose in row.

"Son," Papa didn't yell, but he said it loud, to make sure he was heard over the cows and branding iron heater. He said it firm. "I don't care if you have to use both hands, your belt, your chin, and take a hold with your teeth. When I expect you to hold on . . . you had better hold on."

Wilder nodded and Papa saw that he did.

Wilder could see that Papa had lost his knife in the battle with the leg. It was risky, but he thought he could still get his knife out of his belt holster and hand it to Papa to finish the castration. So, while blocking and holding the leg with his entire torso, he inched his hand over to his knife, spun the long, fixed blade in one hand so as to give it to Papa handle first, and without looking up all the way, poked Papa in the ribs with it.

Papa looked down and saw the silent, but perceptive offering. He smiled and then grabbed it from Wilder and said out loud to no one in particular, "I like a ready man."

Wilder was hurting. His pride and everything physical throbbed with fresh wounds from the beating the calf had just given him.

But still he smiled as he stared at the ground from two inches away.

Papa sliced through the scrotum in one cut as the sharp blade parted the hair and skin with ease. Wilder knew his new knife was getting bloody, and he liked that.

In a final insult from the calf, as each job finished and they moved to let him up, his nasty, poop-covered tail twitched right into Wilder's face. Wilder drew in his lips too late, and helplessly he realized he was now tasting calf manure. His only thought, oddly, was that it tasted green, somehow, as he spit repeatedly.

Wilder wiped his mouth on his sleeve, which wasn't much cleaner than his face. Red, never one to miss a chance, hollered down at him, "Hey Wilder, did you know that stuff makes an excellent chapstick?"

Wilder gave him a puzzled look.

"OK, I'm not certain about that . . . but you'll sure stop licking your lips." Red laughed out loud, and everyone else did, too.

The work went on for another two hours. By the time they finished, Wilder had worked his way through all the jobs and hadn't let any other calves get loose. He was exhausted. The last calf was an especially big heifer, maybe 450 pounds, which had been escaping loops all morning and finally got worked when Red and Artemio head-and-heeled it and stretched it out. Wilder administered the two vaccines and positioned himself near Mark, who was holding the front half down. As the enormous calf pulled Cotton up from the ground, Wilder jumped on its back and gripped his knuckles deep into its hide. All the men watched as the calf bucked and sprinted for the herd. Wilder dug his heels in and held on tight, but the heifer darted sideways at the herd, leaving Wilder in a pile in the dust.

He got up and walked back to the men, who were laughing again. He kind of waddled side to side in the heavy chaps and spurs and riding boots. He sported an ominous black eye now, to match the one Papa had. He was covered in brown and green so that it almost looked like he was wearing camouflage. There was a big rip on the upper sleeve of his denim pearl snap shirt where a sharp Angus hoof had slashed it; it hung open, revealing a large triangle of pale bicep. Dehorning blood had squirted across his chaps and hat making long lines of small solid circles, which pleased Wilder, as the blood would leave a nice, dark stain on leather and felt. Artemio patted him on the back, which raised a dust cloud, and said, “Good ride.”

Wilder’s tired, dirty face grew into a grin.

He looked up at the men and then glanced off into the distance and said to no one in particular, "I sure like brandings."

It was after two o'clock when the famished men headed to the house for lunch. Marisol had grilled ribeye steaks piled high on a platter. They were rare and bloody, which is the way men who know and raise beef eat them. She had stacks of corn and white flour tortillas steaming next to a pot of spicy pinto beans. There was a fresh spinach salad with pecans and strawberries, green chile enchiladas, peach cobbler, and a two-gallon pitcher of iced tea. The more Wilder ate, the hungrier he felt . . . for the first two plates. He just kept stuffing it in like it was going into a bag hidden somewhere under his shirt.

They ate the huge lunch in silence—five hungry men and a boy eating a warm meal they had truly earned.

The work wasn't quite done, so the stuffed men waddled back to the pens to keep from falling asleep. Everybody but Wilder had to adjust their belts. Red bragged on Marisol's cooking, saying he was "full as a tick." Their still-saddled horses nickered as they approached and remounted.

Before they had gone in for lunch, Papa had directed Wilder to turn the calves and mamas back together so that the bawling and separated pairs could find each other and survey the damage. The calves were all next to their mamas, and most were sucking milk greedily. Wilder threw open the gate, and the riders trailed the herd, relaxed and lazy now, back to the west bodark pasture where they had started the morning.

After all the jokes and retelling of the events from the shade of the front porch, Mark and Cotton jumped their saddled horses into their trailer, followed by Red and Artemio into theirs, and they all drove away. Papa and Wilder stood in the dirt driveway and watched them rattle over the cattle guards on the way out.

“Papa, do you think I might own this ranch someday?”

Wilder hadn’t intended to say that, and felt immediately embarrassed and knew he shouldn’t have asked. It was just that his heart, in that moment of contentment and joy, had bubbled over, and the words sort of fell out of his mouth. Words that he had said to himself so many times.

“Papa, I’m sorry, that’s none of my business. I didn’t mean to say that.”

Papa ignored the question, but said this, which was his answer, anyway, “Always remember this Wilder—nobody owns the land.

Anybody who thinks he does is a fool. We are only stewards for little chunks of time, and the luckiest people in the world to be allowed to do that. It's our job to care of the land and preserve it."

Wilder nodded, and Papa continued, "I don't figure we can improve it, but we better not make it worse."

CHAPTER TWELVE

Tell Me Your Adventure

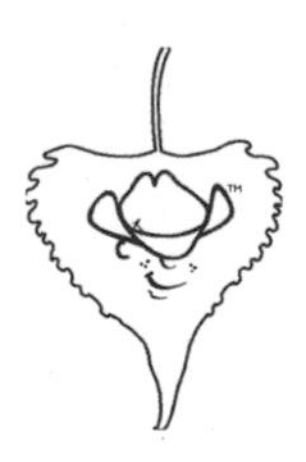

The next morning, Wilder was due back at the bus station, but he awoke to hear Papa banging around, throwing something in the garage. He quickly packed his things and went to see what Papa was doing. He left his new knife dirty with blood (and left it that way in its leather scabbard for the next week, knowing the blood would stain the blade and cow bone handle). Now it had some age; now it was tested.

Papa was chucking white packages of frozen meat from the garage freezer into the trunk of Grandma's black Cadillac. Papa loaded package after package of steaks, hamburger, and roasts, Black Angus beef that the ranch had produced. Three cardboard boxes sat in the open trunk wrapped in blankets. Papa looked up at Wilder and asked him if he was ready to go. Wilder nodded without asking any questions.

"Well, get in." Papa motioned to the car as if Wilder should have known he was riding to the bus station in it. He opened the back door and tossed in his bags, which landed on his mother's saddle, which was another surprise. He sat down on the cushy leather of the front seat. It was quite a difference from the pickup he had been riding in all week. The car smelled like women's perfume. There was a *Cowpokes* by Ace Reid peel-and-stick calendar on the dash. The month showing was from seven years ago, and Wilder figured it was the last his grandmother had seen.

Papa slammed the trunk and got in and didn't say anything for the next eight hours as he drove Wilder through Verbena, past the bus station in Amarillo, and all the way home to Colorado. When they were 30 minutes from Wilder's house, Papa, trying to acknowledge the pain shared between them, croaked out, "You know, I talk to your mom almost every day, Wilder. But to you—how does she look?"

Wilder said she was fine, as much as he knew, and shrugged his shoulders a bit, surprised by the question, but relieved in a way. He knew she wasn't "fine" exactly, and so did Papa, but he was glad to have something said about it.

Papa nodded.

They pulled into the mismatched lot that held the Goods' older trailer house, which contrasted with the tidy landscaping and mature trees. Livy and Molly came out on the porch to greet them in the evening light. Papa and Wilder stood there side by side, both with black eyes. Wilder hugged Livy first, and she inhaled deeply. Even after the one bath he had taken all week, last night, there was still plenty of Texas on him, and it made her smile. Papa hugged Molly warmly and then scooped up his hundred-pound daughter in his arms like a baby calf. He carried her inside and began to cry silent, old man tears.

Wilder grabbed Molly's arm and led her around the side of the house to the backyard. The chickens noticed them from their coop and clucked a few times, which seemed like a friendly "hello." The children sat down beneath the massive cottonwood tree they had always played under. It was so big they couldn't touch hands around the trunk.

"What's wrong with Papa, Wilder? Did you do something? Did you get in a fight? You both have black eyes."

"No, silly, I didn't do anything," Wilder shot back. "I think he just misses Grandma and Momma, that's all."

"Ohhh . . . well, Momma's fine. She told me all about it. Me and Cille had the best time, and

Gale wondered what you were doing all week. He was grumpy."

"Momma's fine, then?"

"Yes, that's what she told me. She doesn't have to go back to Denver for a long time."

Wilder nodded, looking up at the stars that were poking out now in the black sky through the bare limbs of the tree—musing to himself at the difference between the two worlds he had just floated in and out of—realizing he was back in the old one again. A world—and a life—that had already begun to feel foreign in just a week.

"Well, what did you do? Tell me your adventure," Molly begged.

"Too much stuff happened to even tell you, Flopsy," Wilder began (using his pet name for her), smug like always, but knowing he would eventually walk her through all of it.

"I know a bunch of secrets about the ranch that you don't know," Wilder teased.

"Like what?"

"I know how Momma got her name."

"Really!? How?"

"And I have this." Wilder reached into his jeans pocket and spilled out a round tube of five 100-dollar bills.

Molly's eyes broke wide open and her mouth

dropped—not that she knew what 500 dollars really meant, other than it was something they had never seen before. Molly opened the bills and played with them on the dead, brown grass.

Wilder explained that yesterday after the branding Papa had told him to get a shovel and dig carefully under a mesquite knot he placed at the base of a thicket of sand-hill plums just to the north of the house. He said he would find a steel box in the ground and he was to grab five 100-dollar bills out of it for his wages for the week of work, which was 100 dollars a day—a man's wages for ranch work. So he did, and there it was, and there was a ton more money in the box, too.

When he got back to the house, Papa had told Wilder that that was his little "hidey hole" and was a secret just between the two of them. Papa had said that he felt better putting what he took from the land back into it, which didn't make sense exactly, but it felt better to *him* Wilder figured, which was enough.

"Papa said that's where he keeps his real money, his calf crop money," Wilder said.

What Wilder didn't tell her was that he had also seen an old Colt pistol in the box with a paper tag tied to it. It was a single-action six-shooter, and it was worn and used and seemed to pull Wilder's hand like a magnet. Wilder knew better than to handle it, but he did turn over the tag to see "Wilder" written on it in Papa's flowing script. Wilder kept quiet about it with both Molly and Papa.

"What are you going to do with it all?"

"Just give it to Momma and Dad, I guess. But I can't tell them for a couple of days. Papa said to make sure he was long gone when I showed them. He told me to buy some new jeans.

"And I might buy a little something for Sunny," Wilder added. "But just for getting all my homework from last week."

"What are you going to get?"

"Oh, maybe a necklace."

"You can't buy her a necklace. That's crazy. That would be a girlfriend gift."

"Well . . . I don't know." Wilder mumbled.

Molly folded all the bills up and handed them back to Wilder. Her nine-year-old mind cared little for money beyond its novelty.

"Tell me about Momma's name," she said as she wrapped her jacket a bit tighter and leaned back on the rough tree bark.

"Well, Papa says that when Grandma was pregnant they couldn't think of a good name. That fall, they were branding cattle and Grandma was helping him and running the branding iron, even though she had a big belly by then. She couldn't do a real good job, but she tried, and she put a brand on a little blond calf, and when it jumped, it smudged the brand real bad and burned Papa a bit."

Wilder sucked in his breath.

"Papa said the brand burn cleared his mind from the work for a second and he looked at that smudged mark on the calf kind of funny—like he was seeing it for the first time. Well, the bottom of the tree came out with a little tail that made it look like an "*L*" . . . and Papa saw the name *L - I - V - Y*. All right there in the tree water brand."

Wilder pulled out his new knife with the brand in the handle and traced the lines for Molly as she leaned over to see.

"Do you see it, Flopsy?"

Molly smiled.

"I do see it Wilder. *L - I - V - Y*. Livy. Momma's name."

"Flopsy, that means Momma *is* the brand. She *is* a tree in water," Wilder's eyes shone in the moonlight, "which means we're all going to be just fine."

The lights glowed from the house, and Wilder and Molly heard the sound of Hank tossing frozen meat, like clay bricks being stacked, one package at a time, into the freezer under the carport in the front yard. Brother and sister sat still under their tree for a long time that evening as Wilder retraced the lines of the story that he had lived all week, the deer hunt, the rattlesnake, the branding... and how all he wanted in the world was to saddle up every morning. Papa and Momma were inside still, now drinking an evening cup of coffee. They heard Momma laugh. It was a bright sharp laugh that made them both smile. For while Wilder sat outside and told stories about Papa—Papa sat inside and told stories about him.

THE END

ABOUT THE AUTHOR

S. J. Dahlstrom lives and writes in West Texas with his wife and children. A fifth-generation Texan, S. J. has spent his life "bouncing around" the countryside from New Mexico and Texas, north to Colorado and Montana, and east to Michigan and New York. He is interested in all things outdoors and creative. He writes poetry and hunts deer; he plants wildflowers and breaks horses; he reads Ernest Hemingway and Emily Dickinson and C. S. Lewis.

S. J.'s writing draws on his experiences as a cowboy, husband, father—and as a founder of the Whetstone Boys Ranch in Mountain View, Missouri. He says, "I wrote this story about Wilder Good for kids who grew up in the outdoors and for kids who long for the outdoors . . . working, fishing, hunting; farms, ranches, mountains and prairies. I think all kids want to do these things and go to these places." The Adventures of Wilder Good is his first book series.

You can learn more about S. J. Dahlstrom and join Wilder Good on his adventures when you visit the Wilder Good website, *www.WilderGood.com*, where S. J. encourages readers to 'Be Wilder' and submit photos and stories about their own adventures.

Coming Soon!

#3

THE ADVENTURES OF
WILDER GOOD

WILDER AND SUNNY

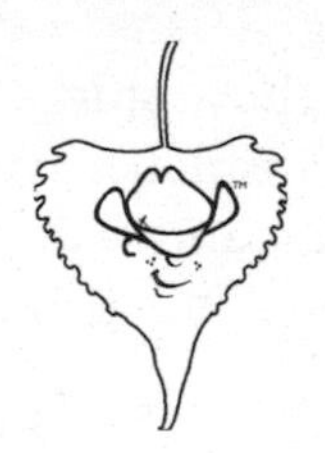